Anton Chekhov

THE DUEL

Anton Chekhov was born in 1860 in southern Russia. The grandson of a serf, he became a physician, paying for his education by selling satirical and humorous sketches to the newspapers. He soon turned to serious short stories, winning the Pushkin Prize in 1887, and went on to write plays, including *Uncle Vanya, The Seagull, Three Sisters,* and *The Cherry Orchard,* and novellas, including *The Steppe* and *The Duel.* He died of tuberculosis in 1904.

ABOUT THE TRANSLATORS

Together, Richard Pevear and Larissa Volokhonsky have translated works by Tolstoy, Dostoevsky, Chekhov, and Gogol. They were twice awarded the PEN/Book-of-the-Month Club Translation Prize (for their versions of Dostoevsky's *The Brothers Karamazov* and Tolstoy's *Anna Karenina*), and their translation of Dostoevsky's *Demons* was one of three nominees for the same prize. They are married and live in France.

Anton Chekhov

THE DUEL

TRANSLATED FROM THE RUSSIAN BY

Richard Pevear and Larissa Volokhonsky

FOREWORD BY *Mary Bing*

INTRODUCTION BY *Richard Pevear*

VINTAGE CLASSICS
Vintage Books
A Division of Random House, Inc.
New York

FIRST VINTAGE CLASSICS EDITION, AUGUST 2010

Library of Congress Cataloging-in-Publication Data
Chekhov, Anton Pavlovich, 1860–1904.
[Duel. English]
The duel / Anton Chekhov ; translated from the Russian by Richard Pevear and Larissa
Volokhonsky ; introduction by Richard Pevear. —1st Vintage Classics ed.
p. cm. —(Vintage classics)
ISBN: 978-0-307-74287-2
I. Pevear, Richard, 1943–   II. Volokhonsky, Larissa.   III. Title.
PG3456.D8P48 2010
891.73'3—dc22
· 2010022386

www.vintagebooks.com

Printed in the United States of America
10 9 8 7 6 5 4 3 2 1

FOREWORD

When he took on the film version of Anton Chekhov's *The Duel*, producer Don Rosenfeld already had literary adaptations under his belt, from his years at Merchant Ivory. This worried me. Would a too-refined sensibility miss Chekhov's broad comedy? Don, however, seemed to understand. "When you squeeze the grape, there has to be juice," he said. We agreed to the respectful mantra of "*Not* Merchant Ivory," and made our first offer, to the most interesting director we could think of.

Werner Herzog turned us down. "Chekhov is not a man to bring to cinema," he said. But Werner, we have pistols! And naked ladies, and midnight trysts, a very public nervous breakdown, and two men at ideological loggerheads, brewing for a fight!

True, "ideological loggerheads" are not cinematic. Even Chekhov fretted to his editor about lack of action in his novella. So why make a movie of *The Duel*?

Because, as Samuel Beckett said, "Nothing is funnier than unhappiness." Laevsky, the story's anti-hero, is a walking disaster, his neuroses the ticking bomb every movie needs. He can't bring himself to marry his mistress, he can't find money to get out of town, and he can't escape himself. "If it goes on for another day or two, I'll strangle myself like . . . like a dog!" he says. Like a dog?

Actors love Chekhov because he gives great direction, right to the spot where internal life rubs up against external reality. We are never who we intend to be. Laevsky, driven mad by his mistress's harmless swallowing at dinner, thinks, "He himself would not kill, of course, but if he had now been on a jury, he would have acquitted the murderer. 'Merci, my dove,' he said after dinner and kissed Nadezhda Fyodorovna on the forehead."

Adulterous Nadya, avid Nadya . . . she is Laevsky's equal in frustration and foolishness. But Chekhov refuses to throw her under the train like Anna Karenina. He enters her dirty mind and discovers innocence. For example: when Laevsky pretends his hysterics were bad digestion; "from time to time, sighing spasmodically, [he] stroked his side as if to show that the pain could still be felt. And nobody except Nadezhda Fyodorovna believed him, and he saw that."

Her self-deception is as devastating as his self-consciousness.

Each page of *The Duel* is lush with revelation. Perceiving it is another matter, as difficult as really listening to a child. Reading Chekhov demands openness, and slowness, and a kind of courage, because reality is harrowing. Here is a young boy at the seaside showing off to his mother and sister: "[He] dove and swam further out, but got tired and hastened back, and by his grave, strained face, one could see that he did not believe in his strength." This minor character never reappears, but his plight—the challenge of being a man among women—resonates through the story.

Chekhov's work has a unique transparence. How on earth did he see inside all of us so clearly? This unveiling becomes easier to grasp—and *The Duel* easier to read—after going to the movie. The actors' full-bodied inhabitation of their roles, their sheer vitality, helps us bear reality. We recognize the characters instantly, since their lies, their delusions, their vivid failures and fantasies are our own.

Ultimately, we root for the anti-hero, because we resemble him more than his opponent, the virtuous zoologist von Koren. As Laevsky says, "Yes, I run up debts, drink, live with another man's wife, I'm hysterical, I'm banal, I'm not as profound as some are, but whose business is that?" This scene, in which

Laevsky inadvertently challenges von Koren to a duel, is riotous, pathetic, and absurd. It is the very vaudeville of our lives.

The Duel isn't about a gunfight; it's about the salvation of souls. Nadya struggles to recover her virtue, but the moral pressure, the stakes, are on the men. Will Laevsky find compassion for the woman he's ruined, or will he abandon her? Will von Koren shoot humanely, or with the violence of the beasts he studies? Will we behave like Man, or Ape? Can religion help?

Chekhov is unabashed in the face of emotion. He touches our largest feelings by the simplest means. When Nadya's entanglements finally make her sick, feverish, Chekhov writes, "She was thirsty, and there was no one to give her a drink." What poor sinner among us has not felt this need, this loneliness, this hopelessness?

Chekhov looks into our dark hearts, and still finds radiance. We read books and watch movies to find this light, to look into these mirrors. If the tools of the twenty-first century stunt our capacity to feel, will our neuroses become obsolete, as von Koren wishes? A world without Laevskys is not funny, it's unimaginable. Perhaps we might leave aside the distractions of speed and screen, to better look at ourselves, and each other. We need Chekhov now more than ever.

The Master can be brutal. Just before Laevsky is about to die, he realizes he wants to live. The end of the novella brings high emotional climax, only to smash-cut to reality. We are back at Beckett's "We can't go on, we must go on." But take heart, Chekhov loves life. *The Duel* is Beckett with great hats. And naked women, and guns that go off, and an absolution that extends to its audience. May we have the grace to take it.

—Mary Bing, screenwriter of the
Flux Films / High Line Pictures film
Anton Chekhov's The Duel, June 2010

INTRODUCTION

Chekhov wrote his first and only novel when he was twenty-four. Its title is *Drama at the Hunt*, translated into English as *A Shooting Party*. It is 170 pages long, was serialized in thirty-two issues of the scandal sheet *Daily News* (which Chekhov renamed *Daily Spews*) from August 1884 to April 1885, and was never reprinted in his lifetime. It is by far his longest work of fiction. As Donald Rayfield wrote in *Chekhov: The Evolution of His Art*, "It reflects almost everything he had ever read, from *The Sorrows of Young Werther* to *The Old Age of Lecoq*. It also contains embryonically everything he was to write." It is part detective story, part psychological study, and very cleverly plotted—a broad parody with a fine sense of the absurd, filled with stock Russian characters and situations, set on a decaying estate that would reappear time and again in Chekhov's subsequent work. One of the characters is a naïve and sympathetic doctor, not unlike Dr. Samoilenko in *The Duel* and some of the other doctors who inhabit Dr. Chekhov's fictional world.

Drama at the Hunt gave fullest expression to Chekhov's early humorous manner, which was otherwise mainly confined to the brief sketches he produced to pay his way through medical school. But through the mid-1890s, before the period of the last great plays, the idea of writing a novel continued to entice him. In February 1894 he took a sizable advance from the Petersburg publisher Adolf Marx ("I've become a Marxist," he would joke later) for a novel to be serialized in the magazine *Niva* ("The Cornfield"). Meanwhile, he was working on what he described to his brother Mikhail as "a novel about Moscow life." This was *Three Years*, a story set in Moscow merchant circles, which he had been mulling over since 1891. It was published early in 1895 in the liberal journal *Russian Thought*. In the spring of 1896, to fulfill his contract with Marx, he set to work on another "novel," eventually entitled *My Life*, his last extended prose work.

Chekhov's genius defined its formal limits in these works of 90 to 120 pages. It balked at anything longer. Literary genres are notoriously elusive of definition (Chekhov called his last play, *The Cherry Orchard*, a comedy; its first director, Konstantin Stanislavsky, considered it a tragedy), but it seems justifiable to call these works short novels, and to distinguish them from Chekhov's other works, which are at most half their length. The question is metrical, not mechanical. A hundred-page narrative, whatever generic title we may give it, moves to a different measure than a narrative of five, or fifteen, or fifty pages. It includes the effective time and space of a full-bodied novel, but treats them with the short story's economy of means. *The Duel* is a masterful example of the genre.

Nikolai Gogol once boasted of *Dead Souls*, "All Russia will appear in it," but later confessed that he had made it all up. The writer who did know and portray "all Russia" was Nikolai Leskov, a slightly younger contemporary of Dostoevsky, Turgenev, and Tolstoy. Leskov had traveled throughout Russia as an agent for the stewards of a rich Russian landowner, sending back reports that delighted his employers and marked his beginnings as a writer. Chekhov never met Dostoevsky or Turgenev; he was invited to Tolstoy's estate only in 1895, when he was already an established writer; but he ran into Leskov at a decisive moment, in the summer of 1883, when he was twenty-three and Leskov fifty-two. After some low-life carousing in Moscow, he and Leskov ended up in a cab together, where, as Chekhov recounted in a letter to his brother, the following exchange took place: "[Leskov] turns to me half drunk and asks: 'Do you know what I am?' 'I do.' 'No, you don't. I'm a mystic.' 'I know.' He stares at me with his old man's popping eyes and prophesies: 'You will die before your brother.' 'Perhaps.' 'I shall anoint you with oil as Samuel did David . . . Write.' "

The consecration was more meaningful than the circumstances suggest. Chekhov was indeed Leskov's successor in important ways, not least in his knowledge of Russia. The critic Boris Eichenbaum wrote: "One of the basic principles of Chekhov's artistic work is the endeavor to embrace all of Russian life in its various manifestations, and not to describe selected spheres, as was customary before him." Dostoevsky was an urban intellectual in excelsis, Turgenev and Tolstoy belonged to the landed gentry, but Chekhov was the son of a former serf, and not only saw things differently but also saw different things than his aristocratic elders. In its linguistic resources—particularly the use of Church Slavonicisms and the rendering of peasant speech—Chekhov's work continues Leskov's. Chekhov also has a paradoxical, Leskovian vision of the harshness and beauty of the world that goes beyond correct moral or ideological attitudes, and he has something of Leskov's deep comic sense. Leskov was an Orthodox Christian, though of a somewhat unorthodox kind, for whom the evil and sin of the world could suddenly be pierced by holiness. Chekhov was an agnostic and a man of science; reason imposed greater restraints on him than on Leskov; but there are moments of transcendence, or near transcendence, in his stories, understated, hedged round with irony, but nevertheless there, when contradiction becomes so intense and unresolvable that the "veil" is almost torn. Donald Rayfield speaks of this "mystic side of Chekhov—his irrational intuition that there is meaning and beauty in the cosmos," and rightly says that it "aligns him more to Leskov than to Tolstoy in the Russian literary tradition." It is also what distinguishes him from Maupassant and Zola, whom he greatly admired.

In 1884, a year after his anointing by Leskov, Chekhov suffered a first hemorrhage of the lungs, revealing the illness that would bear out Leskov's prophecy. He never acknowledged that he was consumptive, though as a doctor he could hardly have mistaken the symptoms. They recurred intermittently but more and more alarmingly in the remaining twenty years of his life. His younger brother, Nikolai, a gifted artist, was also consumptive. His death in June 1889 deeply shocked Chekhov. Two months later, he began writing "A Boring Story," the first-person account of a famous professor of medicine faced with the knowledge of his imminent death and an absolute solitude, detached from everything and everyone around him. The philosopher Lev Shestov considered it "the most autobiographical of all his works." But Shestov is right to insist that the change in Chekhov reflected something more profound than the shock of his brother's death and the awareness that the same fate awaited him. We can only learn what it was from the works that followed, among them *The Duel*, written in 1891. In them impressionism goes from the meteorological to the metaphysical.

In December 1889, Chekhov decided to make a journey across the entire breadth of Russia to Sakhalin Island, off the far eastern coast of Siberia. Given the state of his health, the trip was extremely foolhardy, but he refused to be put off. He was disappointed by the failure of his play *The Wood Demon*, the first version of *Uncle Vanya*, which had opened to boos and catcalls on November 27 and closed immediately; he was generally disgusted with literary life and the role of the fashionable writer; he longed to escape his entanglements with women, editors, theater people, and also to answer his critics, who reproached him with social indifference. He wanted, finally, to do something real. Sakhalin Island was the location of the most notorious prison colony in Russia. He planned to make a detailed survey of conditions on the island and write a report that might help to bring about reforms in the penal system.

After a few months of preparation, reading all he could find about Sakhalin and Siberia, obtaining the necessary permissions, as well as tickets for a return by sea to Odessa, he left on April 21, 1890, traveling by train, riverboat, and covered wagon. Eighty-one days later, on July 11, he set foot on the island, where he spent the next three months gathering information about the prisoners, the guards, their families, the native peoples, the climate, the flora and fauna. He interviewed hundreds of men, women, and children, inspected the mines, the farms, the schools and hospitals (he was especially indignant at the treatment of children and the conditions in the hospitals, and later sent shipments of books and medical supplies to the island). On December 2, 1890, having crossed the China Sea, circumnavigated India, and passed through the Suez Canal and the Bosphorus, he landed in Odessa, bringing with him a pet mongoose and thousands of indexed notecards.

In January he began what would be his longest published work, *Sakhalin Island,* an intentionally dry sociological dissertation, which was completed and appeared serially in *Russian Thought* only, from 1893 to 1894. After his look into the inner abyss in "A Boring Story," he had turned and gone to the worst place on earth, as if to stifle his own metaphysical anguish by plunging into the physical sufferings of others. "Sakhalin," writes Donald Rayfield, "gave Chekhov the first of his experiences of real, irremediable evil . . . in Sakhalin he sensed that social evils and individual unhappiness were inextricably involved; his ethics lost their sharp edge of blame and discrimination."

That experience is reflected, though only indirectly, in *The Duel,* which Chekhov worked on alternately with *Sakhalin Island* during the summer of 1891. The duel it dramatizes, before it becomes literal, is a conflict of ideas between the two main phases of the Russian intelligentsia in the nineteenth century, the liberal idealism of the 1840s and the rational egoism of the 1860s, in the persons of Laevsky, a self-styled "superfluous man" (a type christened by Turgenev in 1850), and von Koren, a zoologist and Social Darwinian with an appropriately

German name. The one talks like a book (or a small library); the other is so dedicated to science that he decides to participate actively in the process of natural selection. Laevsky and von Koren demolish each other in words behind each other's backs, before they face each other with loaded pistols. But it is rather late in the day for dueling, the clash of ideas has grown weary, the situation has degenerated, and the whole thing is displaced from the capitals to a seedy resort town on the Caucasian coast, where the Russians appear as precarious interlopers among the native peoples.

The Duel verges on satire, even farce, but pulls back; it verges on tragedy, but turns comical; it ends by deceiving all our expectations. The closing refrain—"No one knows the real truth"—is first spoken by von Koren, then repeated by Laevsky. Chekhov enters into all his characters' minds in turn. No single point of view prevails.

In *The Duel*, Chekhov's art becomes "polyphonic," but not in the Dostoevskian sense. Dostoevsky's polyphony is built on the genuine dialogue and interpenetration of ideas embodied by his characters—that is, on living contact, on the impossibility of isolated consciousness. In Chekhov, it is exactly the opposite: the idea enters into no relationship with the ideas of others; each consciousness is isolated and impenetrable; there is a polyphony of voices, but no dialogue; there is compassion, but no communion. Chekhov became the master of this protean, quizzical form of narrative, with its radical undercutting of all fixed positions. *The Duel* begins and ends at sea.

In his refusal to force the contradictions of his story to any resolution, Chekhov seems to reach an impasse. But the impasse is not a dead end; it is an opening. The role played in *The Duel* by the beardless young deacon Pobedov (his name comes from the word for victory) is a key to the subtle indirectness of Chekhov's art. And we may remember the moment early in the story when, in a comical reverie, the deacon imagines himself a bishop, intoning the bishop's liturgical prayer:

"Look down from heaven, O God, and behold and visit this vineyard which Thy right hand hath planted." The quality of Chekhov's attention is akin to prayer. Though he was often accused of being indifferent, and sometimes claimed it himself, that is the last thing he was.

—Richard Pevear

THE DUEL

I

IT WAS EIGHT o'clock in the morning—the time when officers, officials, and visitors, after a hot, sultry night, usually took a swim in the sea and then went to the pavilion for coffee or tea. Ivan Andreich Laevsky, a young man about twenty-eight years old, a lean blond, in the peaked cap of the finance ministry[1] and slippers, having come to swim, found many acquaintances on the shore, and among them his friend the army doctor Samoilenko.

With a large, cropped head, neckless, red, big-nosed, with bushy black eyebrows and gray side-whiskers, fat, flabby, and with a hoarse military bass to boot, this Samoilenko made the unpleasant impression of a bully and a blusterer on every newcomer, but two or three days would go by after this first acquaintance, and his face would begin to seem remarkably kind, nice, and even handsome. Despite his clumsiness and slightly rude tone, he was a peaceable man, infinitely kind, good-natured, and responsible. He was on familiar terms with everybody in town, lent money to everybody, treated everybody, made matches, made peace, organized picnics, at which he cooked shashlik and prepared a very tasty mullet soup; he was always soliciting and interceding for someone and always rejoicing over something. According to general opinion, he was sinless and was known to have only two weaknesses: first, he was ashamed of his kindness and tried to mask it with a stern gaze and an assumed rudeness; and second, he liked it when medical assistants and soldiers called him "Your Excellency," though he was only a state councillor.[2]

"Answer me one question, Alexander Davidych," Laevsky began, when the two of them, he and Samoilenko, had gone into the water up to their shoulders. "Let's say you fell in love with a woman and became intimate with her; you lived with her, let's say, for more than two years, and then, as it happens, you fell out of love and began to feel she was a stranger to you. How would you behave in such a case?"

"Very simple. Go, dearie, wherever the wind takes you—and no more talk."

"That's easy to say! But what if she has nowhere to go? She's alone, no family, not a cent, unable to work . . ."

"What, then? Fork her out five hundred, or twenty-five a month—and that's it. Very simple."

"Suppose you've got both the five hundred and the twenty-five a month, but the woman I'm talking about is intelligent and proud. Can you possibly bring yourself to offer her money? And in what form?"

Samoilenko was about to say something, but just then a big wave covered them both, then broke on the shore and noisily rolled back over the small pebbles. The friends went ashore and began to dress.

"Of course, it's tricky living with a woman if you don't love her," Samoilenko said, shaking sand from his boot. "But Vanya, you've got to reason like a human being. If it happened to me, I wouldn't let it show that I'd fallen out of love, I'd live with her till I died."

He suddenly felt ashamed of his words. He caught himself and said:

"Though, for my part, there's no need for women at all. To the hairy devil with them!"

The friends got dressed and went to the pavilion. Here Samoilenko was his own man, and they even reserved a special place for him. Each morning a cup of coffee, a tall cut glass of ice water, and a shot of brandy were served to him on a tray. First he drank the brandy, then the hot coffee, then the ice water, and all that must have been very tasty, because after he drank it, his eyes became unctuous, he smoothed his side-whiskers with both hands, and said, looking at the sea:

"An astonishingly magnificent view!"

After a long night spent in cheerless, useless thoughts, which kept him from sleeping and seemed to increase the sultriness and gloom of the night, Laevsky felt broken and sluggish. Swimming and coffee did not make him any better.

"Let's continue our conversation, Alexander Davidych," he said. "I won't conceal it, I'll tell you frankly, as a friend· things are bad between Nadezhda Fyodorovna and me, very bad! Excuse me for initiating you into my secrets, but I need to speak it out."

Samoilenko, who anticipated what the talk would be about, lowered his eyes and started tapping his fingers on the table.

"I've lived with her for two years and fallen out of love . . ." Laevsky went on. "That is, more precisely, I've realized that there has never been any love . . . These two years were a delusion."

Laevsky had the habit, during a conversation, of studying his pink palms attentively, biting his nails, or crumpling his cuffs with his fingers. And he was doing the same now.

"I know perfectly well that you can't help me," he said, "but I'm talking to you because, for our kind, luckless fellows and superfluous men,[3] talk is the only salvation. I should generalize my every act, I should find an explanation and a justification of my absurd life in somebody's theories, in literary types, in the fact, for instance, that we noblemen are degenerating, and so on . . . Last night, for instance, I comforted myself by thinking all the time: ah, how right Tolstoy is, how pitilessly right! And that made it easier for me. The fact is, brother, he's a great writer! Whatever they say."

Samoilenko, who had never read Tolstoy and was preparing every day to read him, got embarrassed and said:

"Yes, other writers all write from the imagination, but he writes straight from nature."

"My God," sighed Laevsky, "the degree to which we're crippled by civilization! I fell in love with a married woman, and she with me . . . In the beginning it was all kisses, and quiet evenings, and vows, and Spencer,[4] and ideals, and common interests . . . What a lie! Essentially we were running away from her husband, but we lied to ourselves that we were running away from the emptiness of our intelligentsia life. We pictured our future like this: in the beginning, in the Caucasus, while we acquaint ourselves with the place and the people, I'll put on my uniform and serve, then, once we're free to do so, we'll acquire a piece of land, we'll labor in the sweat of our brow, start a vineyard, fields, and so on. If it were you or that zoologist friend of yours, von Koren, instead of me, you'd live with Nadezhda Fyodorovna for maybe thirty years and leave your heirs a rich vineyard and three thousand acres of corn, while I felt bankrupt from the first day. The town is unbearably hot, boring, peopleless, and if you go out to the fields, you imagine venomous centipedes, scorpions, and snakes under every bush and stone, and beyond the fields there are mountains and wilderness. Alien people, alien nature, a pathetic culture—all that, brother, is not as easy as strolling along Nevsky[5] in a fur coat, arm in arm with Nadezhda Fyodorovna, and dreaming about warm lands. What's needed here is a fight to the death, and what sort of fighter am I? A pathetic neurasthenic, an idler . . . From the very first day, I realized that my thoughts about a life of labor and a vineyard weren't worth a damn. As for love, I must tell you that to live with a woman who has read Spencer and followed you to the ends of the earth is as uninteresting as with any Anfisa or Akulina. The same smell of a hot iron, powder, and medications, the same curling papers every morning, and the same self-delusion . . ."

"You can't do without an iron in the household," said Samoilenko, blushing because Laevsky was talking to him so openly about a lady he knew. "I notice you're out of sorts today, Vanya. Nadezhda Fyodorovna is a wonderful, educated woman, you're a man of the greatest intelligence . . . Of course, you're not married," said Samoilenko, turning to look at the neighboring tables, "but that's not your fault, and besides . . . one must be without prejudices and stand on the level of modern ideas. I myself stand for civil marriage, yes . . . But in my opinion, once you're together, you must go on till death."

"Without love?"

"I'll explain to you presently," said Samoilenko. "Some eight years ago there was an agent here, an old man of the greatest intelligence. And this is what he used to say: the main thing in family life is patience. Do you hear, Vanya? Not love but patience. Love can't last long. You lived in love for two years, but now evidently your family life has entered the period when, to preserve the balance, so to speak, you must put all your patience to use . . ."

"You believe your old agent, but for me his advice is meaningless. Your old man could play the hypocrite, he could exercise patience and at the same time look at the unloved person as an object necessary for his exercise, but I haven't fallen so low yet. If I feel a wish to exercise my patience, I'll buy myself some dumbbells or a restive horse, but the person I'll leave in peace."

Samoilenko ordered white wine with ice. When they had each drunk a glass, Laevsky suddenly asked:

"Tell me, please, what does softening of the brain mean?"

"It's . . . how shall I explain to you? . . . a sort of illness, when the brains become softer . . . thin out, as it were."

"Curable?"

"Yes, if the illness hasn't been neglected. Cold showers, Spanish fly . . . Well, something internal."

"So . . . So you see what my position is like. Live with her I cannot: it's beyond my strength. While I'm with you, I philosophize and smile, but at home I completely lose heart. It's so creepy for me that if I were told, let's say, that I had to live with her for even one more month, I think I'd put a bullet in my head. And at the same time, it's impossible to break with her. She's alone, unable to work, I have no money, and neither does she . . . What will she do with herself? Who will she go to? I can't come up with anything . . . Well, so tell me: what's to be done?"

"Mm–yes . . ." growled Samoilenko, not knowing how to reply. "Does she love you?"

"Yes, she loves me to the extent that, at her age and with her temperament, she needs a man. It would be as hard for her to part with me as with powder or curling papers. I'm a necessary component of her boudoir."

Samoilenko was embarrassed.

"You're out of sorts today, Vanya," he said. "You must have slept badly."

"Yes, I did . . . Generally, brother, I feel lousy. My head's empty, my heartbeat's irregular, there's some sort of weakness . . . I've got to escape!"

"Where to?"

"There, to the north. To the pines, to the mushrooms, to people, to ideas . . . I'd give half my life to be somewhere in the province of Moscow or Tula right now, swimming in a little river, getting chilled, you know, then wandering around for a good three hours with the worst of students, chattering away . . . And the smell of hay! Remember? And in the evenings, when you stroll in the garden, the sounds of a piano come from the house, you hear a train going by . . ."

Laevsky laughed with pleasure, tears welled up in his eyes, and, to conceal them, he reached to the next table for matches without getting up.

"And it's eighteen years since I've been to Russia," said

Samoilenko. "I've forgotten how it is there. In my opinion, there's no place in the world more magnificent than the Caucasus."

"Vereshchagin[6] has a painting: two men condemned to death languish at the bottom of a deep well. Your magnificent Caucasus looks to me exactly like that well. If I were offered one of two things, to be a chimney sweep in Petersburg or a prince here, I'd take the post of chimney sweep."

Laevsky fell to thinking. Looking at his bent body, at his eyes fixed on one spot, at his pale, sweaty face and sunken temples, his bitten nails, and the slipper run down at the heel, revealing a poorly darned sock, Samoilenko was filled with pity and, probably because Laevsky reminded him of a helpless child, asked:

"Is your mother living?"

"Yes, but she and I have parted ways. She couldn't forgive me this liaison."

Samoilenko liked his friend. He saw in Laevsky a good fellow, a student, an easygoing man with whom one could have a drink and a laugh and a heart-to-heart talk. What he understood in him, he greatly disliked. Laevsky drank a great deal and not at the right time, played cards, despised his job, lived beyond his means, often used indecent expressions in conversation, went about in slippers, and quarreled with Nadezhda Fyodorovna in front of strangers—and that Samoilenko did not like. But the fact that Laevsky had once been a philology student, now subscribed to two thick journals, often spoke so cleverly that only a few people understood him, lived with an intelligent woman—all this Samoilenko did not understand, and he liked that, and he considered Laevsky above him, and respected him.

"One more detail," said Laevsky, tossing his head. "Only this is between you and me. So far I've kept it from Nadezhda Fyodorovna, don't blurt it out in front of her . . . Two days ago I received a letter saying that her husband has died of a softening of the brain."

"God rest his soul . . ." sighed Samoilenko. "Why are you keeping it from her?"

"To show her this letter would mean: let's kindly go to church and get married. But we have to clarify our relations first. Once she's convinced that we can't go on living together, I'll show her the letter. It will be safe then."

"You know what, Vanya?" said Samoilenko, and his face suddenly assumed a sad and pleading expression, as if he was about to ask for something very sweet and was afraid he would be refused. "Marry her, dear heart!"

"What for?"

"Fulfill your duty before that wonderful woman! Her husband has died, and so Providence itself is showing you what to do!"

"But understand, you odd fellow, that it's impossible. To marry without love is as mean and unworthy of a human being as to serve a liturgy without believing."

"But it's your duty!"

"Why is it my duty?" Laevsky asked with annoyance.

"Because you took her away from her husband and assumed responsibility for her."

"But I'm telling you in plain Russian: I don't love her!"

"Well, so there's no love, then respect her, indulge her . . ."

"Respect her, indulge her . . ." Laevsky parroted. "As if she's a mother superior . . . You're a poor psychologist and physiologist if you think that, living with a woman, you can get by with nothing but deference and respect. A woman needs the bedroom first of all."

"Vanya, Vanya . . ." Samoilenko was embarrassed.

"You're an old little boy, a theoretician, while I'm a young old man and a practician, and we'll never understand each other. Better let's stop this conversation. Mustafa!" Laevsky called out to the waiter. "How much do we owe you?"

"No, no . . ." the doctor was alarmed, seizing Laevsky by the hand. "I'll pay it. I did the ordering. Put it on my account!" he called to Mustafa.

The friends got up and silently walked along the embankment. At the entrance to the boulevard they stopped and shook hands on parting.

"You're much too spoiled, gentlemen!" sighed Samoilenko. "Fate has sent you a young woman, beautiful, educated—and you don't want her, but if God just gave me some lopsided old woman, provided she was gentle and kind, how pleased I'd be! I'd live with her in my little vineyard and . . ."

Samoilenko caught himself and said:

"And the old witch would serve the samovar there."

Having taken leave of Laevsky, he walked down the boulevard. When, corpulent, majestic, a stern expression on his face, in his snow-white tunic and perfectly polished boots, his chest thrust out, adorned by a Vladimir with a bow,[7] he went down the boulevard, for that time he liked himself very much, and it seemed to him that the whole world looked at him with pleasure. Not turning his head, he kept glancing from side to side and found that the boulevard was perfectly well organized, that the young cypresses, eucalyptuses, and scrawny, unattractive palm trees were very beautiful and would, with time, afford ample shade; that the Circassians were an honest and hospitable people. "Strange that Laevsky doesn't like the Caucasus," he thought, "very strange." Five soldiers with rifles passed by and saluted him. On the sidewalk to the right side of the boulevard walked the wife of an official with her schoolboy son.

"Good morning, Marya Konstantinovna!" Samoilenko called out to her, smiling pleasantly. "Have you been for a swim? Ha, ha, ha . . . My respects to Nikodim Alexandrych!"

And he walked on, still smiling pleasantly, but, seeing an army medic coming towards him, he suddenly frowned, stopped him, and asked:

"Is there anyone in the infirmary?"

"No one, Your Excellency."

"Eh?"

"No one, Your Excellency."

"Very well, on your way..."

Swaying majestically, he made for a lemonade stand, where an old, full-breasted Jewess who passed herself off as a Georgian sat behind the counter, and said to her as loudly as if he was commanding a regiment:

"Be so kind as to give me a soda water!"

II

LAEVSKY'S DISLIKE OF Nadezhda Fyodorovna expressed itself chiefly in the fact that everything she said or did seemed to him a lie or the semblance of a lie, and that everything he read against women and love seemed to him to go perfectly with himself, Nadezhda Fyodorovna, and her husband. When he came back home, she was sitting by the window, already dressed and with her hair done, drinking coffee with a preoccupied face and leafing through an issue of a thick journal, and he thought that drinking coffee was not such a remarkable event that one should make a preoccupied face at it, and that she need not have spent time on a modish hairdo, because there was no one there to attract and no reason for doing so. In the issue of the journal, he saw a lie as well. He thought she had dressed and done her hair in order to appear beautiful and was reading the journal in order to appear intelligent.

"Is it all right if I go for a swim today?" she asked.

"Why not! I suppose it won't cause an earthquake whether you do or don't go..."

"No, I'm asking because the doctor might get angry."

"Well, so ask the doctor. I'm not a doctor."

This time what Laevsky disliked most of all in Nadezhda Fyodorovna was her white, open neck and the little curls of hair on her nape, and he remembered that Anna Karenina, when she stopped loving her husband, disliked his ears first of all, and he thought: "How right that is! How right!" Feeling weak and empty in the head, he went to his study, lay down on the sofa, and covered his face with a handkerchief so as not to be bothered by flies. Sluggish, viscous thoughts, all about the same thing, dragged through his brain like a long wagon train on a rainy autumnal day, and he lapsed into a drowsy, oppressed state. It seemed to him that he was guilty before Nadezhda Fyodorovna and before her husband, and that he was to blame for her husband's death. It seemed to him that he was guilty before his own life, which he had ruined, before the world of lofty ideas, knowledge, and labor, and that this wonderful world appeared possible and existent to him not here on this shore, where hungry Turks and lazy Abkhazians wandered about, but there, in the north, where there were operas, theaters, newspapers, and all forms of intellectual work. One could be honest, intelligent, lofty, and pure only there, not here. He accused himself of having no ideals or guiding idea in his life, though now he vaguely understood what that meant. Two years ago, when he had fallen in love with Nadezhda Fyodorovna, it had seemed to him that he had only to take up with Nadezhda Fyodorovna and leave with her for the Caucasus to be saved from the banality and emptiness of life; so now, too, he was certain that he had only to abandon Nadezhda Fyodorovna and leave for Petersburg to have everything he wanted.

"To escape!" he murmured, sitting up and biting his nails. "To escape!"

His imagination portrayed him getting on a steamer, then having breakfast, drinking cold beer, talking with the ladies on deck, then getting on a train in Sebastopol and going. Hello, freedom! Stations flash by one after another, the air turns ever colder and harsher, here are birches and firs, here is Kursk, Moscow . . . In the buffets, cabbage soup, lamb with kasha, sturgeon, beer, in short, no more Asiaticism, but Russia, real Russia. The passengers on the train talk about trade, new singers, Franco-Russian sympathies; everywhere you feel living, cultured, intelligent, vibrant life . . . Faster, faster! Here, finally, is Nevsky, Bolshaya Morskaya, and here is Kovensky Lane, where he once used to live with the students, here is the dear gray sky, the drizzling rain, the wet cabs . . .

"Ivan Andreich!" someone called from the next room. "Are you at home?"

"I'm here!" Laevsky responded. "What do you want?"

"Papers!"

Laevsky got up lazily, with a spinning head, and, yawning and dragging on his slippers, went to the next room. Outside, at the open window, stood one of his young colleagues laying out official papers on the windowsill.

"One moment, my dear boy," Laevsky said softly and went to look for an inkstand; coming back to the window, he signed the papers without reading them and said: "Hot!"

"Yes, sir. Will you be coming today?"

"Hardly . . . I'm a bit unwell. Tell Sheshkovsky, my dear boy, that I'll stop by to see him after dinner."

The clerk left. Laevsky lay down on the sofa again and began to think:

"So, I must weigh all the circumstances and consider. Before leaving here, I must pay my debts. I owe around two thousand roubles. I have no money . . . That, of course, is not important; I'll pay part of it now somehow and send part of it later from Petersburg. The main thing is Nadezhda Fyodorovna . . . First of all, we must clarify our relations . . . Yes."

A little later, he considered: hadn't he better go to Samoilenko for advice?

I could go, he thought, but what use will it be? Again

I'll speak inappropriately about the boudoir, about women, about what's honest or dishonest. Devil take it, what talk can there be here about honest or dishonest if I have to save my life quickly, if I'm suffocating in this cursed captivity and killing myself? . . . It must finally be understood that to go on with a life like mine is meanness and cruelty, before which everything else is petty and insignificant. "To escape!" he murmured, sitting up. "To escape!"

The deserted seashore, the relentless heat, and the monotony of the smoky purple mountains, eternally the same and silent, eternally solitary, aroused his anguish and, it seemed, lulled him to sleep and robbed him. Maybe he was very intelligent, talented, remarkably honest; maybe, if he weren't locked in on all sides by the sea and the mountains, he would make an excellent zemstvo activist,[8] a statesman, an orator, a publicist, a zealot. Who knows! If so, wasn't it stupid to discuss whether it was honest or dishonest if a gifted and useful man, a musician or an artist, for example, breaks through the wall and deceives his jailers in order to escape from captivity? In the position of such a man, everything is honest.

At two o'clock Laevsky and Nadezhda Fyodorovna sat down to dinner. When the cook served them rice soup with tomatoes, Laevsky said:

"The same thing every day. Why not make cabbage soup?"

"There's no cabbage."

"Strange. At Samoilenko's they make cabbage soup, and Marya Konstantinovna has cabbage soup, I alone am obliged for some reason to eat this sweetish slop. It's impossible, my dove."

As happens with the immense majority of spouses, formerly not a single dinner went by for Laevsky and Nadezhda Fyodorovna without caprices and scenes, but ever since Laevsky had decided that he no longer loved her, he had tried to yield to Nadezhda Fyodorovna in everything, spoke gently and politely to her, smiled, called her "my dove."

"This soup tastes like licorice," he said, smiling; he forced himself to appear affable, but he could not restrain himself and said: "Nobody looks after the household here . . . If you're so sick or busy reading, then, if you please, I'll take care of our cooking."

Formerly she would have replied: "Go ahead" or: "I see you want to make a cook out of me," but now she only glanced at him timidly and blushed.

"Well, how are you feeling today?" he asked affectionately.

"Not bad today. Just a little weak."

"You must take care of yourself, my dove. I'm terribly afraid for you."

Nadezhda Fyodorovna was sick with something. Samoilenko said she had undulant fever and gave her quinine; the other doctor, Ustimovich, a tall, lean, unsociable man who sat at home during the day and, in the evening, putting his hands behind him and holding his cane up along his spine, quietly strolled on the embankment and coughed, thought she had a feminine ailment and prescribed warm compresses. Formerly, when Laevsky loved her, Nadezhda Fyodorovna's ailment had aroused pity and fear in him, but now he saw a lie in the ailment as well. The yellow, sleepy face, the listless gaze and fits of yawning that Nadezhda Fyodorovna had after the attacks of fever, and the fact that she lay under a plaid during the attack and looked more like a boy than a woman, and that her room was stuffy and smelled bad—all this, in his opinion, destroyed the illusion and was a protest against love and marriage.

For the second course he was served spinach with hard-boiled eggs, while Nadezhda Fyodorovna, being sick, had custard with milk. When, with a preoccupied face, she first prodded the custard with her spoon and then began lazily eating it, sipping milk along with it, and he heard her swallow, such a heavy hatred came over him that his head even began to itch. He was aware that such a feeling would be insulting even to a dog, but he was vexed not with himself but with Nadezhda Fyodorovna for arousing this feeling in him, and he understood why lovers sometimes kill their mistresses. He himself would not kill, of course, but if he had now been on a jury, he would have acquitted the murderer.

"Merci, my dove," he said after dinner and kissed Nadezhda Fyodorovna on the forehead.

Going to his study, he paced up and down for five minutes, looking askance at his boots, then sat down on the sofa and muttered:

"To escape, to escape! To clarify our relations and escape!"

He lay down on the sofa and again remembered that he was perhaps to blame for the death of Nadezhda Fyodorovna's husband.

"To blame a man for falling in love or falling out of love is stupid," he persuaded himself as he lay there and raised his feet in order to put on his boots. "Love and hate are not in our power. As for the husband, perhaps in an indirect way I was one of the causes of his death, but, again, am I to blame that I fell in love with his wife and she with me?"

Then he got up and, finding his peaked cap, took himself to his colleague Sheshkovsky's, where officials gathered each day to play vint and drink cold beer.

"In my indecision I am reminiscent of Hamlet," Laevsky thought on the way. "How rightly Shakespeare observed it! Ah, how rightly!"

III

SO AS NOT to be bored and to condescend to the extreme need of newcomers and the familyless who, for lack of hotels in the town, had nowhere to dine, Dr. Samoilenko kept something like a table d'hôte in his home. At the time of writing, he had only two people at his table: the young zoologist von Koren, who came to the Black Sea in the summers to study the embryology of jellyfish; and the deacon Pobedov, recently graduated from the seminary and sent to our town to take over the functions of the old deacon, who had gone away for a cure. They each paid twelve roubles a month for dinner and supper, and Samoilenko made them give their word of honor that they would appear for dinner at precisely two o'clock.

Von Koren was usually the first to come. He would sit silently in the drawing room and, taking an album from the table, begin studying attentively the faded photographs of some unknown men in wide trousers and top hats and ladies in crinolines and caps. Samoilenko remembered only a few of them by name, and of those he had forgotten he said with a sigh: "An excellent man, of the greatest intelligence!" Having finished with the album, von Koren would take a pistol from the shelf and, squinting his left eye, aim for a long time at the portrait of Prince Vorontsov, or station himself in front of the mirror and study his swarthy face, big forehead, and hair black and curly as a Negro's, and his faded cotton shirt with large flowers, which resembled a Persian carpet, and the wide leather belt he wore instead of a waistcoat. Self-contemplation afforded him hardly less pleasure than looking at the photographs or the pistol in its costly mounting. He was very pleased with his face, and his handsomely trimmed little beard, and his broad shoulders, which served as obvious proof of his good health and sturdy build. He was also pleased with his smart outfit, starting with the tie, picked to match the color of the shirt, and ending with the yellow shoes.

While he was studying the album and standing in front of the mirror, at the same time, in the kitchen and around it, in the hall, Samoilenko, with no frock coat or waistcoat, bare-chested, excited, and drenched in sweat, fussed about the tables, preparing a salad, or some sort of sauce, or meat, cucumbers, and onions for a cold kvass soup, meanwhile angrily rolling his eyes at the orderly who was helping him, and brandishing a knife or a spoon at him.

"Give me the vinegar!" he ordered. "I mean, not the vinegar but the olive oil!" he shouted, stamping his feet. "Where are you going, you brute?"

"For the oil, Your Excellency," the nonplussed orderly said in a cracked tenor.

"Be quick! It's in the cupboard! And tell Darya to add some dill to the jar of pickles! Dill! Cover the sour cream, you gawk, or the flies will get into it!"

The whole house seemed to resound with his voice. When it was ten or fifteen minutes before two, the deacon would come, a young man of about twenty-two, lean, long-haired, beardless, and with a barely noticeable mustache. Coming into the drawing room, he would cross himself in front of the icon, smile, and offer von Koren his hand.

"Greetings," the zoologist would say coldly. "Where have you been?"

"On the pier fishing for bullheads."

"Well, of course... Apparently, Deacon, you're never going to take up any work."

"Why so? Work's not a bear, it won't run off to the woods," the deacon would say, smiling and putting his hands into the deep pockets of his cassock.

"Beating's too good for you!" the zoologist would sigh.

Another fifteen or twenty minutes would go by, but dinner was not announced, and they could still hear the orderly, his boots stomping, running from the hall to the kitchen and back, and Samoilenko shouting:

"Put it on the table! Where are you shoving it? Wash it first!"

Hungry by now, the deacon and von Koren would start

drumming their heels on the floor, expressing their impatience, like spectators in the gallery of a theater. At last the door would open, and the exhausted orderly would announce: "Dinner's ready!" In the dining room they were met by the crimson and irate Samoilenko, stewed in the stifling kitchen. He looked at them spitefully and, with an expression of terror on his face, lifted the lid of the soup tureen and poured them each a plateful, and only when he had made sure that they were eating with appetite and liked the food did he sigh with relief and sit down in his deep armchair. His face became languid, unctuous . . . He unhurriedly poured himself a glass of vodka and said:

"To the health of the younger generation!"

After his conversation with Laevsky, all the time from morning till dinner, despite his excellent spirits, Samoilenko felt a slight oppression in the depths of his soul. He felt sorry for Laevsky and wanted to help him. Having drunk a glass of vodka before the soup, he sighed and said:

"I saw Vanya Laevsky today. The fellow's having a hard time of it. The material side of his life is inauspicious, but above all, he's beset by psychology. I feel sorry for the lad."

"There's one person I don't feel sorry for!" said von Koren. "If the dear chap were drowning, I'd help him along with a stick: drown, brother, drown . . ."

"Not true. You wouldn't do that."

"Why don't you think so?" the zoologist shrugged his shoulders. "I'm as capable of a good deed as you are."

"Is drowning a man a good deed?" the deacon asked and laughed.

"Laevsky? Yes."

"This kvass soup seems to lack something . . ." said Samoilenko, wishing to change the subject.

"Laevsky is unquestionably harmful and as dangerous for society as the cholera microbe," von Koren went on. "Drowning him would be meritorious."

"It's no credit to you that you speak that way of your neighbor. Tell me, what makes you hate him?"

"Don't talk nonsense, Doctor. To hate and despise a microbe is stupid, but to consider anyone who comes along without discrimination as your neighbor—that, I humbly thank you, that means not to reason, to renounce a just attitude towards people, to wash your hands, in short. I consider your Laevsky a scoundrel, I don't conceal it, and I treat him like a scoundrel in good conscience. Well, but you consider him your neighbor—so go and kiss him; you consider him your neighbor, and that means you have the same relation to him as to me and the deacon—that is, none at all. You're equally indifferent to everybody."

"To call a man a scoundrel!" Samoilenko murmured, wincing scornfully. "That's so wrong, I can't even tell you!"

"One judges people by their actions," von Koren went on. "So judge now, Deacon . . . I shall talk to you, Deacon. The activity of Mr. Laevsky is openly unrolled before you like a long Chinese scroll, and you can read it from beginning to end. What has he done in the two years he's been living here? Let's count on our fingers. First, he has taught the town inhabitants to play vint; two years ago the game was unknown here, but now everybody plays vint from morning till night, even women and adolescents; second, he has taught the townspeople to drink beer, which was also unknown here; to him they also owe a knowledge of various kinds of vodka, so that they can now tell Koshelev's from Smirnov's No. 21 blindfolded. Third, before, they lived with other men's wives here secretly, for the same motives that thieves steal secretly and not openly; adultery was considered something that it was shameful to expose to general view; Laevsky appears to be a pioneer in that respect: he lives openly with another man's wife. Fourth . . ."

Von Koren quickly ate his kvass soup and handed the plate to the orderly.

"I understood Laevsky in the very first month of our acquaintance," he went on, addressing the deacon. "We arrived here at the same time. People like him are very fond of friendship, intimacy, solidarity, and the like, because they always need company for vint, drinking, and eating; besides, they're babblers and need an audience. We became friends, that is, he loafed about my place every day, preventing me from working and indulging in confidences about his kept woman. From the very first, he struck me with his extraordinary falseness, which simply made me sick. In the quality of a friend, I chided him, asking why he drank so much, why he lived beyond his means and ran up debts, why he did nothing and read nothing, why he had so little culture and so little knowledge, and in answer to all my questions, he would smile bitterly, sigh, and say: 'I'm a luckless fellow, a superfluous man,' or 'What do you want, old boy, from us remnants of serfdom,' or 'We're degenerating...' Or he would start pouring out some lengthy drivel about Onegin, Pechorin, Byron's Cain, Bazarov,[9] of whom he said: 'They are our fathers in flesh and spirit.' Meaning he is not to blame that official packets lie unopened for weeks and that he drinks and gets others to drink, but the blame goes to Onegin, Pechorin, and Turgenev, who invented the luckless fellow and the superfluous man. The cause of extreme licentiousness and outrageousness, as you see, lies not in him but somewhere outside, in space. And besides—clever trick!— it's not he alone who is dissolute, false, and vile, but we... 'we, the people of the eighties,' 'we, the sluggish and nervous spawn of serfdom,' 'civilization has crippled us...' In short, we should understand that such a great man as Laevsky is also great in his fall; that his dissoluteness, ignorance, and unscrupulousness constitute a natural-historical phenomenon, sanctified by necessity; that the causes here are cosmic, elemental, and Laevsky should have an icon lamp hung before him, because he is a fatal victim of the times, the trends, heredity, and the rest. All the officials and ladies oh'd and ah'd, listening to him, but I couldn't understand for a long time whom I was dealing with: a cynic or a clever huckster. Subjects like him, who look intelligent, are slightly educated, and talk a lot about their own nobility, can pretend to be extraordinarily complex natures."

"Quiet!" Samoilenko flared up. "I won't allow bad things to be said in my presence about a very noble man!"

"Don't interrupt, Alexander Davidych," von Koren said coldly. "I'll finish presently. Laevsky is a rather uncomplicated organism. Here is his moral structure: in the morning, slippers, bathing, and coffee; then up till dinner, slippers, constitutional, and talk; at two o'clock, slippers, dinner, and drink; at five o'clock, bathing, tea, and drink, then vint and lying; at ten o'clock, supper and drink; and after midnight, sleep and *la femme*. His existence is confined within this tight program like an egg in its shell. Whether he walks, sits, gets angry, writes, rejoices—everything comes down to drink, cards, slippers, and women. Women play a fatal, overwhelming role in his life. He himself tells us that at the age of thirteen, he was already in love; when he was a first-year student, he lived with a lady who had a beneficial influence on him and to whom he owes his musical education. In his second year, he bought out a prostitute from a brothel and raised her to his level—that is, kept her—but she lived with him for about half a year and fled back to her madam, and this flight caused him no little mental suffering. Alas, he suffered so much that he had to leave the university and live at home for two years, doing nothing. But that was for the better. At home he got involved with a widow who advised him to leave the law department and study philology. And so he did. On finishing his studies, he fell passionately in love with his present . . . what's her name? . . . the married one, and had to run away with her here to the Caucasus, supposedly in pursuit of ideals . . . Any day now he'll fall out of love with her and flee back to Petersburg, also in pursuit of ideals."

"How do you know?" Samoilenko growled, looking at the zoologist with spite. "Better just eat."

Poached mullet with Polish sauce was served. Samoilenko placed a whole mullet on each of his boarders' plates and poured the sauce over it with his own hands. A couple of minutes passed in silence.

"Women play an essential role in every man's life," said the deacon. "There's nothing to be done about it."

"Yes, but to what degree? For each of us, woman is a mother, a sister, a wife, a friend, but for Laevsky, she is all that—and at the same time only a mistress. She—that is, cohabiting with her—is the happiness and goal of his life; he is merry, sad, dull, disappointed—on account of a woman; he's sick of his life—it's the woman's fault; the dawn of a new life breaks, ideals are found—look for a woman here as well . . . He's only satisfied by those writings or paintings that have a woman in them. Our age, in his opinion, is bad and worse than the forties and the sixties only because we are unable to give ourselves with self-abandon to amorous ecstasy and passion. These sensualists must have a special growth in their brain, like a sarcoma, that presses on the brain and controls their whole psychology. Try observing Laevsky when he's sitting somewhere in society. You'll notice that when, in his presence, you raise some general question, for instance about cells or instincts, he sits to one side, doesn't speak or listen; he has a languid, disappointed air, nothing interests him, it's all banal and worthless; but as soon as you start talking about males and females, about the fact, for instance, that the female spider eats the male after fertilization, his eyes light up with curiosity, his face brightens, and, in short, the man revives! All his thoughts, however noble, lofty, or disinterested, always have one and the same point of common convergence. You walk down the street with him and meet, say, a donkey... 'Tell me, please,' he asks, 'what would happen if a female donkey was coupled with a camel?' And his dreams! Has he told you his dreams? It's magnificent! Now he dreams he's marrying the moon, then that he's summoned by the police, and there they order him to live with a guitar..."

The deacon burst into ringing laughter; Samoilenko frowned and wrinkled his face angrily, so as not to laugh, but could not help himself and guffawed.

"That's all lies!" he said, wiping his tears. "By God, it's lies!"

IV

THE DEACON WAS much given to laughter and laughed at every trifle till his sides ached, till he dropped. It looked as though he liked being among people only because they had funny qualities and could be given funny nicknames. Samoilenko he called "the tarantula," his orderly "the drake," and he was delighted when von Koren once called Laevsky and Nadezhda Fyodorovna "macaques." He peered greedily into people's faces, listened without blinking, and you could see his eyes fill with laughter and his face strain in anticipation of the moment when he could let himself go and rock with laughter.

"He's a corrupted and perverted subject," the zoologist went on, and the deacon, in anticipation of funny words, fastened his eyes on him. "It's not everywhere you can meet such a nonentity. His body is limp, feeble, and old, and in his intellect he in no way differs from a fat merchant's wife, who only feeds, guzzles, sleeps on a featherbed, and keeps her coachman as a lover."

The deacon guffawed again.

"Don't laugh, Deacon," said von Koren, "it's stupid,

finally. I'd pay no attention to this nonentity," he went on, after waiting for the deacon to stop guffawing, "I'd pass him by, if he weren't so harmful and dangerous. His harmfulness consists first of all in the fact that he has success with women and thus threatens to have progeny, that is, to give the world a dozen Laevskys as feeble and perverted as himself. Second, he's contagious in the highest degree. I've already told you about the vint and the beer. Another year or two and he'll conquer the whole Caucasian coast. You know to what degree the masses, especially their middle stratum, believe in the intelligentsia, in university education, in highborn manners and literary speech. Whatever vileness he may commit, everyone will believe that it's good, that it should be so, since he is an intellectual, a liberal, and a university man. Besides, he's a luckless fellow, a superfluous man, a neurasthenic, a victim of the times, and that means he's allowed to do anything. He's a sweet lad, a good soul, he's so genuinely tolerant of human weaknesses; he's complaisant, yielding, obliging, he's not proud, you can drink with him, and use foul language, and gossip a bit . . . The masses, always inclined to anthropomorphism in religion and morality, like most of all these little idols that have the same weaknesses as themselves. Consider, then, what a wide field for contagion! Besides, he's not a bad actor, he's a clever hypocrite, and he knows perfectly well what o'clock it is. Take his dodges and tricks—his attitude to civilization, for instance. He has no notion of civilization, and yet: 'Ah, how crippled we are by civilization! Ah, how I envy the savages, those children of nature, who know no civilization!' We're to understand, you see, that once upon a time he devoted himself heart and soul to civilization, served it, comprehended it thoroughly, but it exhausted, disappointed, deceived him; you see, he's a Faust, a second Tolstoy . . . He treats Schopenhauer[10] and Spencer like little boys and gives them a fatherly slap on the shoulder: 'Well, how's things, Spencer, old boy?' He hasn't read

Spencer, of course, but how sweet he is when he says of his lady, with a slight, careless irony: 'She's read Spencer!' And people listen to him, and nobody wants to understand that this charlatan has no right not only to speak of Spencer in that tone but merely to kiss Spencer's bootsole! Undermining civilization, authority, other people's altars, slinging mud, winking at them like a buffoon only in order to justify and conceal one's feebleness and moral squalor, is possible only for a vain, mean, and vile brute."

"I don't know what you want from him, Kolya," said Samoilenko, looking at the zoologist now not with anger but guiltily. "He's the same as everybody. Of course, he's not without weaknesses, but he stands on the level of modern ideas, he serves, he's useful to his fatherland. Ten years ago an old man served as an agent here, a man of the greatest intelligence... He used to say..."

"Come, come!" the zoologist interrupted. "You say he serves. But how does he serve? Have the ways here become better and the officials more efficient, more honest and polite, because he appeared? On the contrary, by his authority as an intellectual, university man, he only sanctions their indiscipline. He's usually efficient only on the twentieth, when he receives his salary, and on the other days he only shuffles around the house in slippers and tries to make it look as if he's doing the Russian government a great favor by living in the Caucasus. No, Alexander Davidych, don't defend him. You're insincere from start to finish. If you actually loved him and considered him your neighbor, first of all you wouldn't be indifferent to his weaknesses, you wouldn't indulge them, but would try, for his own good, to render him harmless."

"That is?"

"Render him harmless. Since he's incorrigible, there's only one way he can be rendered harmless..."

Von Koren drew a finger across his neck.

"Or drown him, maybe..." he added. "In the interests of mankind and in their own interests, such people should be destroyed. Without fail."

"What are you saying?" Samoilenko murmured, getting up and looking with astonishment at the zoologist's calm, cold face. "Deacon, what is he saying? Are you in your right mind?"

"I don't insist on the death penalty," said von Koren. "If that has been proved harmful, think up something else. It's impossible to destroy Laevsky—well, then isolate him, depersonalize him, send him to common labor..."

"What are you saying?" Samoilenko was horrified. "With pepper, with pepper!" he shouted in a desperate voice, noticing that the deacon was eating his stuffed zucchini without pepper. "You, a man of the greatest intelligence, what are you saying?! To send our friend, a proud man, an intellectual, to common labor!!"

"And if he's proud and starts to resist—clap him in irons!"

Samoilenko could no longer utter a single word and only twisted his fingers; the deacon looked at his stunned, truly ridiculous face and burst out laughing.

"Let's stop talking about it," the zoologist said. "Remember only one thing, Alexander Davidych, that primitive mankind was protected from the likes of Laevsky by the struggle for existence and selection; but nowadays our culture has considerably weakened the struggle and the selection, and we ourselves must take care of destroying the feeble and unfit, or else, as the Laevskys multiply, civilization will perish and mankind will become totally degenerate. It will be our fault."

"If it comes to drowning and hanging people," said Samoilenko, "then to hell with your civilization, to hell with mankind! To hell! I'll tell you this: you're a man of the greatest learning and intelligence, and the pride of our fatherland, but you've been spoiled by the Germans. Yes, the Germans! The Germans!"

Since leaving Dorpat,[11] where he had studied medicine, Samoilenko had seldom seen Germans and had not read a single German book, but in his opinion, all the evil in politics and science proceeded from the Germans. Where he had acquired such an opinion, he himself was unable to say, but he held fast to it.

"Yes, the Germans!" he repeated once more. "Let's go and have tea."

The three men got up, put on their hats, went to the front garden, and sat down there under the shade of pale maples, pear trees, and a chestnut. The zoologist and the deacon sat on a bench near a little table, and Samoilenko lowered himself into a wicker chair with a broad, sloping back. The orderly brought tea, preserves, and a bottle of syrup.

It was very hot, about ninety-two in the shade. The torrid air congealed, unmoving, and a long spiderweb, dangling from the chestnut to the ground, hung slackly and did not stir.

The deacon took up the guitar that always lay on the ground by the table, tuned it, and began to sing in a soft, thin little voice: " 'Seminary youths stood nigh the pot-house...' " but at once fell silent from the heat, wiped the sweat from his brow, and looked up at the hot blue sky. Samoilenko dozed off; the torrid heat, the silence, and the sweet after-dinner drowsiness that quickly came over all his members left him weak and drunk; his arms hung down, his eyes grew small, his head lolled on his chest. He looked at von Koren and the deacon with tearful tenderness and murmured:

"The younger generation... A star of science and a luminary of the Church... This long-skirted alleluia may someday pop up as a metropolitan,[12] for all I know, I may have to kiss his hand... So what... God grant it..."

Soon snoring was heard. Von Koren and the deacon finished their tea and went out to the street.

"Going back to the pier to fish for bullheads?" asked the zoologist.

"No, it's too hot."

"Let's go to my place. You can wrap a parcel for me and do some copying. Incidentally, we can discuss what you're going to do with yourself. You must work, Deacon. It's impossible like this."

"Your words are just and logical," said the deacon, "but my laziness finds its excuse in the circumstances of my present life. You know yourself that an uncertainty of position contributes significantly to people's apathy. God alone knows whether I've been sent here for a time or forever; I live here in uncertainty, while my wife languishes at her father's and misses me. And, I confess, my brains have melted from the heat."

"That's all nonsense," said the zoologist. "You can get used to the heat, and you can get used to being without a wife. It won't do to pamper yourself. You must keep yourself in hand."

v

NADEZHDA FYODOROVNA WAS going to swim in the morning, followed by her kitchen maid, Olga, who was carrying a jug, a copper basin, towels, and a sponge. Two unfamiliar steamships with dirty white stacks stood at anchor in the roads, evidently foreign freighters. Some men in white, with white shoes, were walking about the pier and shouting loudly in French, and answering calls came from the ships. The bells were ringing briskly in the small town church.

"Today is Sunday!" Nadezhda Fyodorovna recalled with pleasure.

She felt perfectly well and was in a gay, festive mood. Wearing a new loose dress of coarse man's tussore and a big straw hat, its wide brim bent down sharply to her ears, so that her face looked out of it as if out of a box, she fancied herself very sweet. She was thinking that in the whole town there was only one young, beautiful, intelligent woman—herself—and that she alone knew how to dress cheaply, elegantly, and with taste. For example, this dress had cost only twenty-two roubles, and yet how sweet it was! In the whole town, she alone could still attract men, and there were many, and there-fore, willy-nilly, they should all envy Laevsky.

She was glad that lately Laevsky had been cold, politely restrained, and at times even impertinent and rude with her; to all his outbursts and all his scornful, cold, or strange, incomprehensible glances, she would formerly have re-sponded with tears, reproaches, and threats to leave him, or to starve herself to death, but now her response was merely to blush, to glance at him guiltily and be glad that he was not nice to her. If he rebuked her or threatened her, it would be still better and more agreeable, because she felt herself roundly guilty before him. It seemed to her that she was guilty, first, because she did not sympathize with his dreams of a life of labor, for the sake of which he had abandoned Petersburg and come here to the Caucasus, and she was certain that he had been cross with her lately precisely for that. As she was going to the Caucasus, it had seemed to her that on the very first day, she would find there a secluded nook on the coast, a cozy garden with shade, birds, brooks, where she could plant flowers and vegetables, raise ducks and chickens, receive neighbors, treat poor muzhiks and dis-tribute books to them; but it turned out that the Caucasus was bare mountains, forests, and enormous valleys, where you had to spend a long time choosing, bustling about, build-ing, and that there weren't any neighbors there, and it was very hot, and they could be robbed. Laevsky was in no rush to acquire a plot; she was glad of that, and it was as if they both agreed mentally never to mention the life of labor. He was silent, she thought, that meant he was angry with her for being silent.

Second, over those two years, unknown to him, she had bought all sorts of trifles in Atchmianov's shop for as much as three hundred roubles. She had bought now a bit of fabric, then some silk, then an umbrella, and the debt had imperceptibly mounted.

"I'll tell him about it today . . ." she decided, but at once realized that, given Laevsky's present mood, it was hardly opportune to talk to him about debts.

Third, she had already twice received Kirilin, the police chief, in Laevsky's absence: once in the morning, when Laevsky had gone to swim, and the other time at midnight, when he was playing cards. Remembering it, Nadezhda Fyodorovna flushed all over and turned to look at the kitchen maid, as if fearing she might eavesdrop on her thoughts. The long, unbearably hot, boring days, the beautiful, languorous evenings, the stifling nights, and this whole life, when one did not know from morning to evening how to spend the useless time, and the importunate thoughts that she was the most beautiful young woman in town and that her youth was going for naught, and Laevsky himself, an honest man with ideas, but monotonous, eternally shuffling in his slippers, biting his nails, and boring her with his caprices— resulted in her being gradually overcome with desires, and, like a madwoman, she thought day and night about one and the same thing. In her breathing, in her glance, in the tone of her voice, and in her gait—all she felt was desire; the sound of the sea told her she had to love, so did the evening darkness, so did the mountains . . . And when Kirilin began to court her, she had no strength, she could not and did not want to resist, and she gave herself to him . . .

Now the foreign steamships and people in white reminded her for some reason of a vast hall; along with the French talk, the sounds of a waltz rang in her ears, and her breast trembled with causeless joy. She wanted to dance and speak French.

She reasoned joyfully that there was nothing terrible in her infidelity; her soul took no part in it; she continues to love Laevsky, and that is obvious from the fact that she is jealous of him, pities him, and misses him when he's not at home. Kirilin turned out to be so-so, a bit crude, though handsome; she's broken everything off with him, and there won't be anything more. What there was is past, it's nobody's business, and if Laevsky finds out, he won't believe it.

There was only one bathing cabin on the shore, for women; the men bathed under the open sky. Going into the bathing cabin, Nadezhda Fyodorovna found an older lady there, Marya Konstantinovna Bitiugov, the wife of an official, and her fifteen-year-old daughter, Katya, a schoolgirl; the two were sitting on a bench undressing. Marya Konstantinovna was a kind, rapturous, and genteel person who spoke in a drawl and with pathos. Until the age of thirty-two, she had lived as a governess, then she married the official Bitiugov, a small bald person who brushed his hair forward on his temples and was very placid. She was still in love with him, was jealous, blushed at the word "love," and assured everyone that she was very happy.

"My dear!" she said rapturously, seeing Nadezhda Fyodorovna and giving her face the expression that all her acquaintances called "almond butter." "Darling, how nice that you've come! We'll bathe together—that's charming!"

Olga quickly threw off her dress and chemise and began to undress her mistress.

"The weather's not so hot today as yesterday, isn't that so?" said Nadezhda Fyodorovna, shrinking under the rough touch of the naked kitchen maid. "Yesterday it was so stifling I nearly died."

"Oh, yes, my dear! I nearly suffocated myself. Would you

believe, yesterday I went bathing three times . . . imagine, my
dear, three times! Even Nikodim Alexandrych got worried."

"How can they be so unattractive?" thought Nadezhda
Fyodorovna, glancing at Olga and the official's wife. She
looked at Katya and thought: "The girl's not badly built."

"Your Nikodim Alexandrych is very, very sweet!" she
said. "I'm simply in love with him."

"Ha, ha, ha!" Marya Konstantinovna laughed forcedly.
"That's charming!"

Having freed herself of her clothes, Nadezhda Fyodorovna
felt a wish to fly. And it seemed to her that if she waved her
arms, she would certainly take off. Undressed, she noticed
that Olga was looking squeamishly at her white body. Olga,
married to a young soldier, lived with her lawful husband
and therefore considered herself better and higher than her
mistress. Nadezhda Fyodorovna also felt that Marya Konstantinovna and Katya did not respect her and were afraid of her.
That was unpleasant, and to raise herself in their opinion,
she said:

"It's now the height of the dacha season[13] in Petersburg.
My husband and I have so many acquaintances! We really
must go and visit them."

"It seems your husband's an engineer?" Marya Konstantinovna asked timidly.

"I'm speaking of Laevsky. He has many acquaintances.
But unfortunately his mother, a proud aristocrat, rather
limited . . ."

Nadezhda Fyodorovna did not finish and threw herself
into the water; Marya Konstantinovna and Katya went in
after her.

"Our society has many prejudices," Nadezhda Fyodorovna continued, "and life is not as easy as it seems."

Marya Konstantinovna, who had served as a governess in
aristocratic families and knew something about society, said:

"Oh, yes! Would you believe, at the Garatynskys' it was

absolutely required that one dress both for lunch and for dinner, so that, like an actress, besides my salary, I also received money for my wardrobe."

She placed herself between Nadezhda Fyodorovna and Katya, as if screening her daughter from the water that lapped at Nadezhda Fyodorovna. Through the open door that gave onto the sea, they could see someone swimming about a hundred paces from the bathing cabin.

"Mama, it's our Kostya!" said Katya.

"Ah, ah!" Marya Konstantinovna clucked in fright. "Ah! Kostya," she cried, "go back! Go back, Kostya!"

Kostya, a boy of about fourteen, to show off his bravery before his mother and sister, dove and swam further out, but got tired and hastened back, and by his grave, strained face, one could see that he did not believe in his strength.

"These boys are trouble, darling!" Marya Konstantinovna said, calming down. "He can break his neck any moment. Ah, darling, it's so pleasant and at the same time so difficult to be a mother! One's afraid of everything."

Nadezhda Fyodorovna put on her straw hat and threw herself out into the sea. She swam some thirty feet away and turned on her back. She could see the sea as far as the horizon, the ships, the people on the shore, the town, and all of it, together with the heat and the transparent, caressing waves, stirred her and whispered to her that she must live, live . . . A sailboat raced swiftly past her, energetically cleaving the waves and the air; the man who sat at the tiller looked at her, and she found it pleasing to be looked at . . .

After bathing, the ladies dressed and went off together.

"I have a fever every other day, and yet I don't get thinner," Nadezhda Fyodorovna said, licking her lips, which were salty from bathing, and responding with smiles to the bows of acquaintances. "I've always been plump, and now it seems I'm plumper still."

"That, darling, is a matter of disposition. If someone is

not disposed to plumpness, like me, for instance, no sort of food will help. But darling, you've got your hat all wet."

"Never mind, it will dry."

Nadezhda Fyodorovna again saw people in white walking on the embankment and talking in French; and for some reason, joy again stirred in her breast, and she vaguely remembered some great hall in which she had once danced, or of which, perhaps, she had once dreamed. And something in the very depths of her soul vaguely and dully whispered to her that she was a petty, trite, trashy, worthless woman . . .

Marya Konstantinovna stopped at her gate and invited her to come in for a moment.

"Come in, my dear!" she said in a pleading voice, at the same time looking at Nadezhda Fyodorovna with anguish and hope: maybe she'll refuse and not come in!

"With pleasure," Nadezhda Fyodorovna accepted. "You know how I love calling on you!"

And she went into the house. Marya Konstantinovna seated her, gave her coffee, offered her some sweet rolls, then showed her photographs of her former charges, the young Garatynsky ladies, who were all married now, and also showed her Katya's and Kostya's grades at the examinations; the grades were very good, but to make them look still better, she sighed and complained about how difficult it was now to study in high school . . . She attended to her visitor, and at the same time pitied her, and suffered from the thought that Nadezhda Fyodorovna, by her presence, might have a bad influence on Katya's and Kostya's morals, and she was glad that her Nikodim Alexandrych was not at home. Since, in her opinion, all men liked "such women," Nadezhda Fyodorovna might have a bad influence on Nikodim Alexandrych as well.

As she talked with her visitor, Marya Konstantinovna remembered all the while that there was to be a picnic that evening and that von Koren had insistently asked that the macaques—that is, Laevsky and Nadezhda Fyodorovna—not be told about it, but she accidentally let it slip, turned all red, and said in confusion:

"I hope you'll be there, too!"

VI

THE ARRANGEMENT WAS to go seven miles out of town on the road to the south, stop by the dukhan[14] at the confluence of the two rivers—the Black and the Yellow—and cook fish soup there. They set out shortly after five. At the head of them all, in a charabanc, rode Samoilenko and Laevsky; after them, in a carriage drawn by a troika, came Marya Konstantinovna, Nadezhda Fyodorovna, Katya, and Kostya; with them came a basket of provisions and dishes. In the next equipage rode the police chief Kirilin and the young Atchmianov, the son of that same merchant Atchmianov to whom Nadezhda Fyodorovna owed three hundred roubles, and on a little stool facing them, his legs tucked under, sat Nikodim Alexandrych, small, neat, with his hair brushed forward. Behind them all rode von Koren and the deacon; at the deacon's feet was a basket of fish.

"Keep r-r-right!" Samoilenko shouted at the top of his lungs whenever they met a native cart or an Abkhazian riding a donkey.

"In two years, when I have the means and the people ready, I'll go on an expedition," von Koren was telling the deacon. "I'll follow the coast from Vladivostok to the Bering Straits and then from the Straits to the mouth of the Yenisei. We'll draw a map, study the flora and fauna, and undertake thorough geological, anthropological, and ethnographic investigations. Whether you come with me or not is up to you."

"It's impossible," said the deacon.

"Why?"

"I'm attached, a family man."

"The deaconess will let you go. We'll provide for her. It would be still better if you persuaded her, for the common good, to be tonsured a nun; that would also enable you to be tonsured and join the expedition as a hieromonk.[15] I could arrange it for you."

The deacon was silent.

"Do you know your theology well?" asked the zoologist.

"Poorly."

"Hm ... I can't give you any guidance in that regard, because I have little acquaintance with theology. Give me a list of the books you need, and I'll send them to you from Petersburg in the winter. You'll also have to read the notes of clerical travelers: you sometimes find good ethnographers and connoisseurs of Oriental languages among them. When you've familiarized yourself with their manner, it will be easier for you to set to work. Well, and while there are no books, don't waste time, come to me, and we'll study the compass, go through some meteorology. It's all much needed."

"Maybe so ..." the deacon murmured and laughed. "I've asked for a post in central Russia, and my uncle the archpriest has promised to help me in that. If I go with you, it will turn out that I've bothered him for nothing."

"I don't understand your hesitation. If you go on being an ordinary deacon, who only has to serve on feast days and rests from work all the other days, even after ten years you'll still be the same as you are now; the only addition will be a mustache and a little beard, whereas if you come back from an expedition after the same ten years, you'll be a different man, enriched by the awareness of having accomplished something."

Cries of terror and delight came from the ladies' carriage. The carriages were driving along a road carved into the sheer cliff of the rocky coast, and it seemed to them all that they were riding on a shelf attached to a high wall, and that the carriages were about to fall into the abyss. To the right spread the sea, to the left an uneven brown wall with black spots, red veins, and creeping roots, and above, bending over as if with fear and curiosity, curly evergreens looked down. A minute later, there were shrieks and laughter again: they had to drive under an enormous overhanging rock.

"I don't understand why the devil I'm coming with you," said Laevsky. "How stupid and banal! I need to go north, to escape, to save myself, and for some reason I'm going on this foolish picnic."

"But just look at this panorama!" Samoilenko said to him as the horses turned left, and the valley of the Yellow River came into view, and the river itself glistened—yellow, turbid, mad . . .

"I don't see anything good in it, Sasha," replied Laevsky. "To constantly go into raptures over nature is to show the paucity of your imagination. All these brooks and cliffs are nothing but trash compared to what my imagination can give me."

The carriages were now driving along the riverbank. The high, mountainous banks gradually converged, the valley narrowed, and ahead was what looked like a gorge; the stony mountain they were driving along had been knocked together by nature out of huge stones, which crushed each other with such terrible force that Samoilenko involuntarily grunted each time he looked at them. The somber and beautiful mountain was cut in places by narrow crevices and gorges that breathed dampness and mysteriousness on the travelers; through the gorges, other mountains could be seen, brown, pink, purple, smoky, or flooded with bright light. From time to time, as they drove past the gorges, they could hear water falling from a height somewhere and splashing against the rocks.

"Ah, cursed mountains," sighed Laevsky, "I'm so sick of them!"

At the place where the Black River fell into the Yellow River and its water, black as ink, dirtied the yellow water and struggled with it, the Tartar Kerbalai's dukhan stood by the side of the road, with a Russian flag on the roof and a sign written in chalk: "The Pleasant Dukhan." Next to it was a small garden surrounded by a wattle fence, where tables and benches stood, and a single cypress, beautiful and somber, towered over the pitiful thorny bushes.

Kerbalai, a small, nimble Tartar in a blue shirt and white apron, stood in the road and, holding his stomach, bowed low to the approaching carriages and, smiling, showed his gleaming white teeth.

"Greetings, Kerbalaika!" Samoilenko called out to him. "We'll drive on a little further, and you bring us a samovar and some chairs! Step lively!"

Kerbalai kept nodding his cropped head and muttering something, and only those sitting in the last carriage could hear clearly: "There are trout, Your Excellency!"

"Bring them, bring them!" von Koren said to him.

Having driven some five hundred paces past the dukhan, the carriages stopped. Samoilenko chose a small meadow strewn with stones suitable for sitting on, and where a tree brought down by a storm lay with torn-up, shaggy roots and dry yellow needles. A flimsy log bridge had been thrown across the river at this spot, and on the other bank, just opposite, a shed for drying corn stood on four short pilings, looking like the fairy-tale hut on chicken's legs.[16] A ladder led down from its doorway.

The first impression everyone had was that they would never get out of there. On all sides, wherever one looked, towering mountains loomed up, and the evening shadow was approaching quickly, quickly, from the direction of the dukhan and the somber cypress, and that made the narrow, curved valley of the Black River seem narrower and the mountains higher. One could hear the murmuring of the river and the constant trilling of cicadas.

"Charming!" said Marya Konstantinovna, inhaling deeply with rapture. "Children, see how good it is! What silence!"

"Yes, it is good, in fact," agreed Laevsky, who liked the view and, for some reason, when he looked at the sky and then at the blue smoke coming from the chimney of the dukhan, suddenly grew sad. "Yes, it's good!" he repeated.

"Ivan Andreich, describe this view!" Marya Konstantinovna said tearfully.

"What for?" asked Laevsky. "The impression is better than any description. When writers babble about this wealth of colors and sounds that we all receive from nature by way of impressions, they make it ugly and unrecognizable."

"Do they?" von Koren asked coldly, choosing for himself the biggest stone by the water and trying to climb up and sit on it. "Do they?" he repeated, staring fixedly at Laevsky. "And Romeo and Juliet? And Pushkin's Ukrainian night,[17] for instance? Nature should come and bow down at its feet."

"Perhaps..." agreed Laevsky, too lazy to reason and object. "However," he said a little later, "what are Romeo and Juliet essentially? A beautiful, poetic, sacred love rww under which they want to hide the rot. Romeo is the same animal as everyone else."

"Whatever one talks with you about, you always bring it all down to..."

Von Koren looked at Katya and did not finish.

"What do I bring it down to?" asked Laevsky.

"Somebody says to you, for instance, 'How beautiful is a bunch of grapes!' and you say, 'Yes, but how ugly when it's chewed and digested in the stomach.' Why say that? It's not new and... generally, it's a strange manner you have."

Laevsky knew that von Koren did not like him, and he was therefore afraid of him and felt in his presence as if they were all crowded together and somebody was standing behind his back. He said nothing in reply, walked away, and regretted that he had come.

"Gentlemen, off you go to fetch brush for the fire!" commanded Samoilenko.

They all wandered off at random, and the only ones who stayed put were Kirilin, Atchmianov, and Nikodim Alexandrych. Kerbalai brought chairs, spread a rug on the ground, and set down several bottles of wine. The police chief, Kirilin, a tall, imposing man who wore an overcoat over his tunic in all weather, with his haughty bearing, pompous stride, and thick, somewhat rasping voice, resembled all provincial police chiefs of the younger generation. His expression was sad and sleepy, as though he had just been awakened against his wishes.

"What is this you've brought, you brute?" he asked Kerbalai, slowly enunciating each word. "I told you to serve Kvareli, and what have you brought, you Tartar mug? Eh? What?"

"We have a lot of wine of our own, Egor Alexeich," Nikodim Alexandrych observed timidly and politely.

"What, sir? But I want my wine to be there, too. I'm taking part in the picnic, and I presume I have every right to contribute my share. I pre-sume! Bring ten bottles of Kvareli!"

"Why so many?" Nikodim Alexandrych, who knew that Kirilin had no money, was surprised.

"Twenty bottles! Thirty!" cried Kirilin.

"Never mind, let him!" Atchmianov whispered to Nikodim Alexandrych. "I'll pay."

Nadezhda Fyodorovna was in a gay, mischievous mood. She wanted to leap, laugh, exclaim, tease, flirt. In her cheap calico dress with blue flecks, red shoes, and the same straw hat, it seemed to her that she was small, simple, light and airy as a butterfly. She ran out on the flimsy bridge and looked into the water for a moment to make herself dizzy, then cried out and, laughing, ran across to the drying shed, and it seemed to her that all the men, even Kerbalai, admired her. When, in the swiftly falling darkness, the trees were merging with the mountains, the horses with the carriages, and a little light shone in the windows of the dukhan, she climbed a path that wound up the mountainside between the stones and thorny bushes and sat on a stone. Below, the fire was already burning. Near the fire, the deacon moved with rolled-up sleeves, and his long black shadow circled radius-like around the flames. He kept putting on more brush and stirring the pot with a spoon tied to a long stick. Samoilenko, with a copper-red face, bustled about the fire as in his own kitchen and shouted fiercely:

"Where's the salt, gentlemen? Did you forget it? Why are you all sitting around like landowners, and I'm the only one bustling about?"

Laevsky and Nikodim Alexandrych sat next to each other on the fallen tree and gazed pensively at the fire. Marya Konstantinovna, Katya, and Kostya were taking the tea service and plates out of the baskets. Von Koren, his arms crossed and one foot placed on a stone, stood on the bank just beside the water and thought about something. Red patches from the fire, together with shadows, moved on the ground near the dark human figures, trembled on the mountainside, on the trees, on the bridge, on the drying shed; on the other side, the steep, eroded bank was all lit up, flickered, and was reflected in the river, and the swift-running, turbulent water tore its reflection to pieces.

The deacon went for the fish, which Kerbalai was cleaning and washing on the bank, but halfway there, he stopped and looked around.

"My God, how good!" he thought. "The people, the stones, the fire, the twilight, the ugly tree—nothing more, but how good!"

On the far bank, by the drying shed, some unknown

people appeared. Because the light flickered and the smoke from the fire was carried to the other side, it was impossible to make out these people all at once, but they caught glimpses now of a shaggy hat and a gray beard, now of a blue shirt, now of rags hanging from shoulders to knees and a dagger across the stomach, now of a swarthy young face with black brows, as thick and bold as if they had been drawn with charcoal. About five of them sat down on the ground in a circle, while the other five went to the drying shed. One stood in the doorway with his back to the fire and, putting his hands behind him, began telling something that must have been very interesting, because, when Samoilenko added more brush and the fire blazed up, spraying sparks and brightly illuminating the drying barn, two physiognomies could be seen looking out the door, calm, expressing deep attention, and the ones sitting in a circle also turned and began listening to the story. A little later, the ones sitting in a circle began softly singing something drawn-out, melodious, like church singing during Lent . . . Listening to them, the deacon imagined how it would be with him in ten years, when he came back from the expedition: a young hiero-monk, a missionary, an author with a name and a splendid past; he is ordained archimandrite, then bishop; he serves the liturgy in a cathedral; in a golden mitre with a panagia, he comes out to the ambo and, blessing the mass of people with the trikíri and dikíri, proclaims: "Look down from heaven, O God, and behold and visit this vineyard which Thy right hand hath planted!" And the children's angelic voices sing in response: "Holy God . . ."[18]

"Where's the fish, Deacon?" Samoilenko's voice rang out.

Returning to the fire, the deacon imagined a procession with the cross going down a dusty road on a hot July day; at the head the muzhiks carry banners, and the women and girls icons; after them come choirboys and a beadle with a bandaged cheek and straw in his hair; then, in due order, himself, the deacon, after him a priest in a skull cap and with a cross, and behind them, raising dust, comes a crowd of muzhiks, women, boys; there, in the crowd, are the priest's wife and the deaconess, with kerchiefs on their heads. The choir sings, babies howl, quails call, a lark pours out its song... Now they stop and sprinkle a herd with holy water... Go further, and on bended knee pray for rain. Then a bite to eat, conversation...

"And that, too, is good..." thought the deacon.

VII

KIRILIN AND ATCHMIANOV were climbing the path up the mountainside. Atchmianov lagged behind and stopped, and Kirilin came up to Nadezhda Fyodorovna.

"Good evening!" he said, saluting her.

"Good evening."

"Yes, ma'am!" Kirilin said, looking up at the sky and thinking.

"Why 'Yes, ma'am'?" asked Nadezhda Fyodorovna after some silence, and noticed that Atchmianov was watching the two of them.

"And so," the officer pronounced slowly, "our love withered away before it had time to flower, so to speak. How am I to understand that? Is it coquetry on your part, or do you regard me as a scapegrace with whom you can act however you please?"

"It was a mistake! Leave me alone!" Nadezhda Fyodorovna said sharply, looking at him with fear on that beautiful, wonderful evening, and asking herself in perplexity if there could indeed have been a moment when she had liked this man and been intimate with him.

"So, ma'am!" said Kirilin. He stood silently for a while, pondering, and said: "What, then? Let's wait till you're in a better mood, and meanwhile, I venture to assure you that I am a respectable man and will not allow anyone to doubt it. I am not to be toyed with! Adieu!"

He saluted her and walked off, making his way through the bushes. A little later, Atchmianov approached hesitantly.

"A fine evening tonight!" he said with a slight Armenian accent.

He was not bad-looking, dressed according to fashion, had the simple manners of a well-bred young man, but Nadezhda Fyodorovna disliked him because she owed his father three hundred roubles; there was also the unpleasantness of a shop-keeper being invited to the picnic, and the unpleasantness of his having approached her precisely that evening, when her soul felt so pure.

"Generally, the picnic's a success," he said after some silence.

"Yes," she agreed, and as if she had just remembered her debt, she said casually: "Ah, yes, tell them in your shop that Ivan Andreich will come one of these days and pay them the three hundred . . . or I don't remember how much."

"I'm ready to give you another three hundred, if only you'll stop mentioning this debt every day. Why such prose?"

Nadezhda Fyodorovna laughed. The amusing thought came to her head that, if she were immoral enough and wished to, she could get rid of this debt in one minute. If, for instance, she were to turn the head of this handsome young fool! How amusing, absurd, wild it would be indeed! And she suddenly wanted to make him fall in love with her, to fleece him, to drop him, and then see what would come of it.

"Allow me to give you one piece of advice," Atchmianov said timidly. "Beware of Kirilin, I beg you. He tells terrible things about you everywhere."

"I'm not interested in knowing what every fool tells about me," Nadezhda Fyodorovna said coldly, and uneasiness came over her, and the amusing thought of toying with the pretty young Atchmianov suddenly lost its charm.

"We must go down," she said. "They're calling."

Down there the fish soup was ready. It was poured into plates and eaten with that religious solemnity which only occurs at picnics. They all found the soup very tasty and said they had never had anything so tasty at home. As happens at all picnics, lost amidst a mass of napkins, packets, needless greasy wrappings scudding about in the wind, no one knew which glass and which piece of bread was whose, they poured wine on the rug and on their knees, spilled salt, and it was dark around them, and the fire burned less brightly, and they were all too lazy to get up and put on more brush. They all drank wine, and Kostya and Katya got half a glass each. Nadezhda Fyodorovna drank a glass, then another, became drunk, and forgot about Kirilin.

"A splendid picnic, a charming evening," said Laevsky, made merry by the wine, "but I'd prefer a nice winter to all this. 'A frosty dust silvers his beaver collar.'"[19]

"Tastes vary," observed von Koren.

Laevsky felt awkward: the heat of the fire struck him in the back, and von Koren's hatred in the front and face; this hatred from a decent, intelligent man, which probably concealed a substantial reason, humiliated him, weakened him, and, unable to confront it, he said in an ingratiating tone:

"I passionately love nature and regret not being a student of natural science. I envy you."

"Well, and I have no regret or envy," said Nadezhda Fyodorovna. "I don't understand how it's possible to be seriously occupied with bugs and gnats when people are suffering."

Laevsky shared her opinion. He was totally unacquainted with natural science and therefore could never reconcile himself to the authoritative tone and learned, profound air

47

of people who studied the feelers of ants and the legs of cockroaches, and it had always vexed him that, on the basis of feelers, legs, and some sort of protoplasm (for some reason, he always imagined it like an oyster), these people should undertake to resolve questions that embraced the origin and life of man. But he heard a ring of falseness in Nadezhda Fyodorovna's words, and he said, only so as to contradict her:

"The point is not in the bugs but in the conclusions!"

VIII

IT WAS LATE, past ten o'clock, when they began getting into the carriages to go home. Everyone settled in, the only ones missing were Nadezhda Fyodorovna and Atchmianov, who were racing each other and laughing on the other side of the river.

"Hurry up, please!" Samoilenko called to them.

"The ladies shouldn't have been given wine," von Koren said in a low voice.

Laevsky, wearied by the picnic, by von Koren's hatred, and by his own thoughts, went to meet Nadezhda Fyodorovna, and when, merry, joyful, feeling light as a feather, breathless and laughing, she seized him by both hands and put her head on his chest, he took a step back and said sternly:

"You behave like a... cocotte."

This came out very rudely, so that he even felt sorry for her. On his angry, tired face she read hatred, pity, vexation with her, and she suddenly lost heart. She realized that she had overdone it, that she had behaved too casually, and, saddened, feeling heavy, fat, coarse, and drunk, she sat in the first empty carriage she found, along with Atchmianov. Laevsky sat with Kirilin, the zoologist with Samoilenko, the deacon with the ladies, and the train set off.

"That's how they are, the macaques . . ." von Koren began, wrapping himself in his cloak and closing his eyes. "Did you hear, she doesn't want to study bugs and gnats because people are suffering. That's how all macaques judge the likes of us. A slavish, deceitful tribe, intimidated by the knout and the fist for ten generations; they tremble, they wax tender, they burn incense only before force, but let a macaque into a free area, where there's nobody to take it by the scruff of the neck, and it loses control and shows its real face. Look how brave it is at art exhibitions, in museums, in theaters, or when it passes judgment on science: it struts, it rears up, it denounces, it criticizes . . . And it's sure to criticize—that's a feature of slaves! Just listen: people of the liberal professions are abused more often than swindlers—that's because three-quarters of society consists of slaves, the same macaques as these. It never happens that a slave offers you his hand and thanks you sincerely for the fact that you work."

"I don't know what you want!" Samoilenko said, yawning. "The poor woman, in her simplicity, wanted to chat with you about something intelligent, and you go drawing conclusions. You're angry with him for something, and also with her just for company. But she's a wonderful woman!"

"Oh, come now! An ordinary kept woman, depraved and banal. Listen, Alexander Davidych, when you meet a simple woman who isn't living with her husband and does nothing but hee-hee-hee and ha-ha-ha, you tell her to go and work. Why are you timid and afraid to tell the truth here? Only because Nadezhda Fyodorovna is kept not by a sailor but by an official?"

"What am I to do with her, then?" Samoilenko became angry. "Beat her or something?"

"Don't flatter vice. We curse vice only out of earshot, but that's like a fig in the pocket.[20] I'm a zoologist, or a sociologist, which is the same thing; you are a doctor; society believes us; it's our duty to point out to it the terrible harm with which it and future generations are threatened by the existence of ladies like this Nadezhda Ivanovna."

"Fyodorovna," Samoilenko corrected. "And what should society do?"

"It? That's its business. In my opinion, the most direct and proper way is force. She ought to be sent to her husband *manu militari*,* and if the husband won't have her, then send her to hard labor or some sort of correctional institution."

"Oof!" sighed Samoilenko. He paused and asked softly: "The other day you said people like Laevsky ought to be destroyed... Tell me, if somehow... suppose the state or society charged you with destroying him, would you... do it?"

"With a steady hand."

IX

RETURNING HOME, LAEVSKY and Nadezhda Fyodorovna went into their dark, dull, stuffy rooms. Both were silent. Laevsky lit a candle, and Nadezhda Fyodorovna sat down and, without taking off her cloak and hat, raised her sad, guilty eyes to him.

He realized that she was expecting a talk from him; but to talk would be boring, useless, and wearisome, and he felt downhearted because he had lost control and been rude to her. He chanced to feel in his pocket the letter he had been wanting to read to her every day, and he thought that if he showed her the letter now, it would turn her attention elsewhere.

"It's time to clarify our relations," he thought. "I'll give it to her, come what may."

He took out the letter and handed it to her.

"Read it. It concerns you."

*By military force.

Having said this, he went to his study and lay down on the sofa in the darkness, without a pillow. Nadezhda Fyodorovna read the letter, and it seemed to her that the ceiling had lowered and the walls had closed in on her. It suddenly became cramped, dark, and frightening. She quickly crossed herself three times and said:

"Give rest, O Lord . . . give rest, O Lord . . ."[21]

And she wept.

"Vanya!" she called. "Ivan Andreich!"

There was no answer. Thinking that Laevsky had come in and was standing behind her chair, she sobbed like a child and said:

"Why didn't you tell me earlier that he had died? I wouldn't have gone on the picnic, I wouldn't have laughed so terribly . . . Men were saying vulgar things to me. What sin, what sin! Save me, Vanya, save me . . . I'm going out of my mind . . . I'm lost . . ."

Laevsky heard her sobs. He felt unbearably suffocated, and his heart was pounding hard. In anguish, he got up, stood in the middle of the room for a while, felt in the darkness for the chair by the table, and sat down.

"This is a prison . . ." he thought. "I must get out . . . I can't . . ."

It was too late to go and play cards, there were no restaurants in the town. He lay down again and stopped his ears so as not to hear the sobbing, and suddenly remembered that he could go to Samoilenko's. To avoid walking past Nadezhda Fyodorovna, he climbed out the window to the garden, got over the fence, and went on down the street. It was dark. Some steamer had just arrived—a big passenger ship, judging by its lights . . . An anchor chain clanked. A small red light moved quickly from the coast to the ship: it was the customs boat.

"The passengers are asleep in their cabins . . ." thought Laevsky, and he envied other people's peace.

The windows of Samoilenko's house were open. Laevsky looked through one of them, then another: it was dark and quiet inside.

"Alexander Davidych, are you asleep?" he called. "Alexander Davidych!"

Coughing was heard, and an anxious cry:

"Who's there? What the devil?"

"It's me, Alexander Davidych. Forgive me."

A little later, a door opened; the soft light of an icon lamp gleamed, and the enormous Samoilenko appeared, all in white and wearing a white nightcap.

"What do you want?" he asked, breathing heavily from being awakened and scratching himself. "Wait, I'll open up at once."

"Don't bother, I'll come in the window..."

Laevsky climbed through the window and, going up to Samoilenko, seized him by the hand.

"Alexander Davidych," he said in a trembling voice, "save me! I beseech you, I adjure you, understand me! My situation is tormenting. If it goes on for another day or two, I'll strangle myself like . . . like a dog!"

"Wait... What exactly are you referring to?"

"Light a candle."

"Ho-hum . . ." sighed Samoilenko, lighting a candle. "My God, my God . . . It's already past one o'clock, brother."

"Forgive me, but I can't stay at home," said Laevsky, feeling greatly relieved by the light and Samoilenko's presence. "You, Alexander Davidych, are my best and only friend... All my hope lies in you. Whether you want to or not, for God's sake, help me out. I must leave here at all costs. Lend me some money!"

"Oh, my God, my God! . . ." Samoilenko sighed, scratching himself. "I'm falling asleep and I hear a whistle—a steamer has come—and then you... How much do you need?"

"At least three hundred roubles. I should leave her a hundred, and I'll need two hundred for my trip . . . I already owe you about four hundred, but I'll send you all of it . . . all of it . . ."

Samoilenko took hold of both his side-whiskers with one hand, stood straddle-legged, and pondered.

"So . . ." he murmured, reflecting. "Three hundred . . . Yes . . . But I haven't got that much. I'll have to borrow it from somebody."

"Borrow it, for God's sake!" said Laevsky, seeing by Samoilenko's face that he wanted to give him the money and was sure to do it. "Borrow it, and I'll be sure to pay it back. I'll send it from Petersburg as soon as I get there. Don't worry about that. Look, Sasha," he said, reviving, "let's have some wine!"

"Wine . . . That's possible."

They both went to the dining room.

"And what about Nadezhda Fyodorovna?" asked Samoilenko, setting three bottles and a plate of peaches on the table. "Can she be staying on?"

"I'll arrange it all, I'll arrange it all . . ." said Laevsky, feeling an unexpected surge of joy. "I'll send her money afterwards, and she'll come to me . . . And then we'll clarify our relations. To your health, friend."

"Wait," said Samoilenko. "Drink this one first . . . It's from my vineyard. This bottle is from Navaridze's vineyard, and this one from Akhatulov's . . . Try all three and tell me frankly . . . Mine seems to be a bit acidic. Eh? Don't you find?"

"Yes. You've really comforted me, Alexander Davidych. Thank you . . . I've revived."

"A bit acidic?"

"Devil knows, I don't know. But you're a splendid, wonderful man!"

Looking at his pale, agitated, kindly face, Samoilenko

remembered von Koren's opinion that such people should be destroyed, and Laevsky seemed to him a weak, defenseless child whom anyone could offend and destroy.

"And when you go, make peace with your mother," he said. "It's not nice."

"Yes, yes, without fail."

They were silent for a while. When they had drunk the first bottle, Samoilenko said:

"Make peace with von Koren as well. You're both most excellent and intelligent people, but you stare at each other like two wolves."

"Yes, he's a most excellent and intelligent man," agreed Laevsky, ready now to praise and forgive everybody. "He's a remarkable man, but it's impossible for me to be friends with him. No! Our natures are too different. I'm sluggish, weak, submissive by nature; I might offer him my hand at a good moment, but he'd turn away from me ... with scorn."

Laevsky sipped some wine, paced from corner to corner, and, stopping in the middle of the room, went on:

"I understand von Koren very well. He's firm, strong, despotic by nature. You've heard him talking constantly about an expedition, and they're not empty words. He needs the desert, a moonlit night; around him in tents and under the open sky sleep his hungry and sick Cossacks, guides, porters, a doctor, a priest, worn out by the difficult marches, and he alone doesn't sleep and, like Stanley,[22] sits in his folding chair and feels himself the king of the desert and master of these people. He walks, and walks, and walks somewhere, his people groan and die one after the other, but he walks and walks, and in the end dies himself, and still remains the despot and king of the desert, because the cross on his grave can be seen by caravans from thirty or forty miles away, and it reigns over the desert. I'm sorry the man is not in military service. He'd make an excellent, brilliant general. He'd know how to drown his cavalry in the river and make bridges from the corpses, and such boldness is more necessary in war than any fortifications or tactics. Oh, I understand him very well! Tell me, why does he eat himself up here? What does he need here?"

"He's studying marine fauna."

"No. No, brother, no!" sighed Laevsky. "I was told by a scientist traveling on the steamer that the Black Sea is poor in fauna, and that organic life is impossible in the depths of it owing to the abundance of hydrogen sulfate. All serious zoologists work at biological stations in Naples or Ville-franche. But von Koren is independent and stubborn: he works on the Black Sea because nobody works here; he's broken with the university, doesn't want to know any scientists and colleagues, because he's first of all a despot and only then a zoologist. And you'll see, something great will come of him. He's already dreaming now that when he returns from the expedition, he'll smoke out the intrigue and mediocrity in our universities and tie the scientists in knots. Despotism is as strong in science as in war. And he's living for the second summer in this stinking little town, because it's better to be first in a village than second in a city.[23] Here he's a king and an eagle; he's got all the inhabitants under his thumb and oppresses them with his authority. He's taken everybody in hand, he interferes in other people's affairs, he wants to be in on everything, and everybody's afraid of him. I'm slipping out from under his paw, he senses it, and he hates me. Didn't he tell you that I should be destroyed or sent to the public works?"

"Yes," laughed Samoilenko.

Laevsky also laughed and drank some wine.

"His ideals are despotic as well," he said, laughing and taking a bite of peach. "Ordinary mortals, if they work for the general benefit, have their neighbor in mind—me, you, in short, a human being. But for von Koren, people are puppies and nonentities, too small to be the goal of his life.

He works, he'll go on an expedition and break his neck there, not in the name of love for his neighbor but in the name of such abstractions as mankind, future generations, an ideal race of people. He worries about the improvement of the human race, and in that respect we are merely slaves for him, cannon fodder, beasts of burden; he'd destroy some or slap them with hard labor, others he'd bind with discipline, like Arakcheev,[24] make them get up and lie down to the drum, set eunuchs to protect our chastity and morality, order that anyone who steps outside the circle of our narrow, conservative morality be shot at, and all that in the name of improving the human race . . . But what is the human race? An illusion, a mirage . . . Despots have always been given to illusions. I understand him very well, brother. I appreciate him and do not deny his significance; this world stands on men like him, and if the world were placed at the disposal of us alone, with all our kindness and good intentions, we'd do with it just what the flies are doing to that painting. It's true."

Laevsky sat down beside Samoilenko and said with genuine enthusiasm:

"I'm an empty, worthless, fallen man! The air I breathe, this wine, love, in short, life—I've been buying it all up to now at the price of lies, idleness, and pusillanimity. Up to now I've been deceiving people and myself, I've suffered from it, and my sufferings have been cheap and trite. I timidly bend my neck before von Koren's hatred, because at times I, too, hate and despise myself."

Laevsky again paced from corner to corner in agitation and said:

"I'm glad I see my shortcomings clearly and am aware of them. That will help me to resurrect and become a different man. My dear heart, if only you knew how passionately, with what anguish, I thirst for my renewal. And I swear to you, I will be a man! I will! I don't know whether it's the wine speaking in me, or it's so in reality, but it seems to me that it's long since I've lived through such bright, pure moments as now with you."

"Time to sleep, brother . . ." said Samoilenko.

"Yes, yes . . . Forgive me. I'll go at once."

Laevsky fussed around the furniture and windows, looking for his cap.

"Thank you . . ." he murmured, sighing. "Thank you . . . Gentleness and a kind word are higher than alms. You've revived me."

He found his cap, stopped, and looked guiltily at Samoilenko.

"Alexander Davidych!" he said in a pleading voice.

"What?"

"Allow me, dear heart, to spend the night with you!"

"Please do . . . why not?"

Laevsky lay down to sleep on the sofa, and for a long time went on talking with the doctor.

X

SOME THREE DAYS after the picnic, Marya Konstantinovna unexpectedly came to Nadezhda Fyodorovna and, without greeting her, without taking off her hat, seized her by both hands, pressed them to her bosom, and said in great agitation:

"My dear, I'm so agitated, so shocked. Our dear, sympathetic doctor told my Nikodim Alexandrych yesterday that your husband has passed away. Tell me, dear . . . Tell me, is it true?"

"Yes, it's true, he died," Nadezhda Fyodorovna answered.

"My dear, it's terrible, terrible! But there's no bad without some good. Your husband was probably a marvelous, wonderful, holy man, and such people are more needed in heaven than on earth."

All the little lines and points in Marya Konstantinovna's

face trembled, as if tiny needles were leaping under her skin. She smiled an almond-butter smile and said rapturously, breathlessly:

"And so you're free, my dear. Now you can hold your head high and look people boldly in the eye. From now on, God and men will bless your union with Ivan Andreich. It's charming. I'm trembling with joy, I can't find words. My dear, I'll be your sponsor... Nikodim Alexandrych and I have loved you so much, you must allow us to bless your lawful, pure union. When, when are you going to be married?"

"I haven't even thought about it," said Nadezhda Fyodorovna, freeing her hands.

"That's impossible, my dear. You have thought about it, you have!"

"By God, I haven't," laughed Nadezhda Fyodorovna. "Why should we get married? I see no need for it. We'll live as we've lived."

"What are you saying!" Marya Konstantinovna was horrified. "For God's sake, what are you saying!"

"If we get married, it won't be any better. On the contrary, even worse. We'll lose our freedom."

"My dear! My dear, what are you saying!" cried Marya Konstantinovna, stepping back and clasping her hands. "You're being extravagant! Come to your senses! Settle down!"

"What do you mean, settle down? I haven't lived yet, and you tell me to settle down!"

Nadezhda Fyodorovna remembered that indeed she had not lived yet. She had finished the girls' institute and married a man she did not love, then she had taken up with Laevsky and had been living with him the whole time on that dull, deserted coast in expectation of something better. Was that life?

"Yet it would be proper to get married..." she thought but, remembering Kirilin and Atchmianov, blushed and said:

"No, it's impossible. Even if Ivan Andreich were to beg me on his knees, even then I would refuse."

Marya Konstantinovna sat silently on the sofa for a moment, sad, serious, looking at a single point, then got up and said coldly:

"Good-bye, my dear! Excuse me for having troubled you. Though it's not easy for me, I must tell you that from this day on, everything is over between us, and despite my deepest respect for Ivan Andreich, the door of my house is closed to you."

She uttered it with solemnity and was crushed herself by her solemn tone; her face trembled again, took on a soft almond-butter expression; she held out both hands to the frightened and abashed Nadezhda Fyodorovna and said imploringly:

"My dear, allow me at least for one minute to be your mother or an older sister! I'll be open with you, like a mother."

Nadezhda Fyodorovna felt such warmth, joy, and compassion for herself in her breast, as though it really was her mother, risen from the dead, who stood before her. She embraced Marya Konstantinovna impulsively and pressed her face to her shoulder. They both wept. They sat down on the sofa and sobbed for a few minutes, not looking at each other and unable to utter a single word.

"My dear, my child," Marya Konstantinovna began, "I shall tell you some stern truths, without sparing you."

"Do, do, for God's sake!"

"Trust me, my dear. You remember, of all the local ladies, I was the only one to receive you. You horrified me from the very first day, but I was unable to treat you with scorn, like everyone else. I suffered for dear, kind Ivan Andreich as for a son. A young man in a strange land, inexperienced, weak, with no mother, and I was tormented, tormented . . . My husband was against making his acquaintance, but

I talked him into it...I persuaded him...We began to receive Ivan Andreich, and you with him, of course, otherwise he would have been insulted. I have a daughter, a son... You understand, the tender mind of a child, the pure heart...and whosoever shall offend one of these little ones[25]...I received you and trembled for my children. Oh, when you're a mother, you'll understand my fear. And everyone was surprised that I received you, forgive me, as a respectable woman, people hinted to me...well, of course, there was gossip, speculation...Deep in my soul, I condemned you, but you were unhappy, pathetic, extravagant, and I suffered out of pity."

"But why? Why?" asked Nadezhda Fyodorovna, trembling all over. "What have I done to anyone?"

"You're a terrible sinner. You broke the vow you gave your husband at the altar. You seduced an excellent young man who, if he hadn't met you, might have taken himself a lawful life's companion from a good family of his circle, and he would now be like everybody else. You've ruined his youth. Don't speak, don't speak, my dear! I will not believe that a man can be to blame for our sins. The women are always to blame. In everyday domestic life, men are frivolous, they live by their minds, not their hearts, there's much they don't understand, but a woman understands everything. Everything depends on her. Much is given her, and much will be asked of her. Oh, my dear, if she were stupider or weaker than man in this respect, God wouldn't have entrusted her with the upbringing of little boys and girls. And then, dearest, you entered upon the path of vice, forgetting all shame; another woman in your position would have hidden herself from people, would have sat locked up at home, and people would have seen her only in God's church, pale, dressed all in black, weeping, and each would say with sincere contrition: 'God, this is a sinful angel returning to you again...' But you, my dear, forgot all modesty, you lived openly, extravagantly, as if you were proud of your sin, you frolicked, you laughed, and looking at you, I trembled with horror, fearing lest a thunderbolt from heaven strike our house while you were sitting with us. My dear, don't speak, don't speak!" Marya Konstantinovna cried, noticing that Nadezhda Fyodorovna was about to speak. "Trust me, I won't deceive you, and I won't conceal a single truth from the eyes of your soul. Listen to me, then, dearest... God marks great sinners, and you have been marked. Remember, your dresses have always been awful!"

Nadezhda Fyodorovna, who had always had the highest opinion of her dresses, stopped crying and looked at her in astonishment.

"Yes, awful!" Marya Konstantinovna went on. "Anyone could judge your behavior by the refinement and showiness of your clothes. Everyone chuckled and shrugged, looking at you, but I suffered, suffered... And forgive me, my dear, but you are slovenly! When I met you in the bathing cabin, you made me tremble. Your dress was still so-so, but the petticoat, the chemise... my dear, I blush! Poor Ivan Andreich has no one to tie his necktie properly, and by the poor man's linen and boots, one can see that no one looks after him at home. And you always keep him hungry, my darling, and indeed, if there's no one at home to see to the coffee and the samovar, willy-nilly, one spends half one's salary in the pavilion. And your home is simply terrible, terrible! Nobody in the whole town has flies, but you can't get rid of them, the plates and saucers are black. On the windows and tables, just look—dust, dead flies, glasses... What are the glasses doing here? And my dear, your table still hasn't been cleared yet. It's a shame to go into your bedroom: underwear lying about, those various rubber things of yours hanging on the walls, certain vessels standing about... My dear! A husband should know nothing, and a wife should be as pure as a little angel before him! I wake up every morning at the first light and wash my face with cold water, so that my Nikodim Alexandrych won't see me looking sleepy."

"That's all trifles," Nadezhda Fyodorovna burst into sobs. "If only I were happy, but I'm so unhappy!"

"Yes, yes, you're very unhappy!" Marya Konstantinovna sighed, barely keeping herself from crying. "And awful grief awaits you in the future! A lonely old age, illnesses, and then your answer before the dread Judgment Seat[26] ... Terrible, terrible! Now fate itself is offering you a helping hand, and you senselessly push it aside. Get married, get married quickly!"

"Yes, I must, I must," said Nadezhda Fyodorovna, "but it's impossible!"

"Why so?"

"Impossible! Oh, if you only knew!"

Nadezhda Fyodorovna was going to tell her about Kirilin, and about how she had met the young, handsome Atchmianov on the pier the previous evening, and how the crazy, funny thought had come into her head of getting rid of her three-hundred-rouble debt, she had found it very funny, and had returned home late at night, feeling irretrievably fallen and sold. She did not know how it happened herself. And now she was about to swear before Marya Konstantinovna that she would repay the debt without fail, but sobs and shame prevented her from speaking.

"I'll go away," she said. "Ivan Andreich can stay, and I'll go away."

"Where?"

"To Russia."

"But how are you going to live? You have nothing."

"I'll do translations or ... or open a little library ..."

"Don't fantasize, my dear. You need money to start a library. Well, I'll leave you now, and you calm down and think, and come to see me tomorrow all cheered up. That will be charming! Well, good-bye, my little angel. Let me kiss you."

Marya Konstantinovna kissed Nadezhda Fyodorovna on the forehead, made a cross over her, and quietly left. It was already growing dark, and Olga lit a light in the kitchen. Still weeping, Nadezhda Fyodorovna went to the bedroom and lay on the bed. She was in a high fever. She undressed lying down, crumpled her clothes towards her feet, and rolled up in a ball under the blanket. She was thirsty, and there was no one to give her a drink.

"I'll pay it back!" she said to herself, and in her delirium it seemed to her that she was sitting by some sick woman and in her recognized herself. "I'll pay it back. It would be stupid to think it was for money that I . . . I'll go away and send him money from Petersburg. First a hundred . . . then a hundred . . . and then another hundred . . ."

Laevsky came late at night.

"First a hundred . . ." Nadezhda Fyodorovna said to him, "then another hundred . . ."

"You should take some quinine," he said and thought: "Tomorrow is Wednesday, the steamer leaves, and I'm not going. That means I'll have to live here till Saturday."

Nadezhda Fyodorovna got up on her knees in bed.

"Did I say anything just now?" she asked, smiling and squinting because of the candle.

"Nothing. We'll have to send for the doctor tomorrow morning. Sleep."

He took a pillow and went to the door. Once he had finally decided to go away and abandon Nadezhda Fyodorovna, she had begun to arouse pity and a feeling of guilt in him; he was slightly ashamed in her presence, as in the presence of an old or ailing horse slated to be killed. He stopped in the doorway and turned to look at her.

"I was annoyed at the picnic and said something rude to you. Forgive me, for God's sake."

Having said this, he went to his study, lay down, and for a long time was unable to fall asleep.

The next morning, when Samoilenko, in full dress uniform with epaulettes and decorations on occasion of the feast day, was coming out of the bedroom after taking Nadezhda Fyodorovna's pulse and examining her tongue, Laevsky, who was standing by the threshold, asked him worriedly:

"Well, so? So?"

His face expressed fear, extreme anxiety, and hope.

"Calm down, it's nothing dangerous," said Samoilenko. "An ordinary fever."

"I'm not asking about that," Laevsky winced impatiently. "Did you get the money?"

"Forgive me, dear heart," Samoilenko whispered, glancing back at the door and getting embarrassed. "For God's sake, forgive me! Nobody has ready cash, and so far I've only collected by fives or tens—a hundred and ten roubles in all. Today I'll talk with someone else. Be patient."

"But Saturday's the last day!" Laevsky whispered, trembling with impatience. "By all that's holy, before Saturday! If I don't leave on Saturday, I'll need nothing... nothing! I don't understand how a doctor can have no money!"

"Thy will be done, O Lord," Samoilenko whispered quickly and tensely, and something even squeaked in his throat, "they've taken everything I've got, I have seven thousand owing to me, and I'm roundly in debt. Is it my fault?"

"So you'll get it by Saturday? Yes?"

"I'll try."

"I beg you, dear heart! So that the money will be in my hands Friday morning."

Samoilenko sat down and wrote a prescription for quinine in a solution of *kalii bromati*, infusion of rhubarb, and *tincturae gentianae aquae foeniculi*—all of it in one mixture, with the addition of rose syrup to remove the bitterness, and left.

XI

"YOU LOOK AS though you're coming to arrest me," said von Koren, seeing Samoilenko coming into his room in full dress uniform.

"I was passing by and thought: why don't I pay a call on zoology?" said Samoilenko, sitting down by the big table the zoologist himself had knocked together out of simple planks. "Greetings, holy father!" he nodded to the deacon, who was sitting by the window copying something. "I'll sit for a minute and then run home to give orders for dinner. It's already time . . . I'm not bothering you?"

"Not at all," replied the zoologist, laying out scraps of paper covered with fine writing on the table. "We're busy copying."

"So . . . Oh, my God, my God . . ." sighed Samoilenko; he cautiously drew from the table a dusty book on which lay a dead, dry phalangid, and said: "However! Imagine some little green bug is going about his business and suddenly meets such an anathema on his way. I can picture how terrifying it is!"

"Yes, I suppose so."

"It's given venom to defend itself from enemies?"

"Yes, to defend itself and to attack."

"So, so, so . . . And everything in nature, my dear hearts, is purposeful and explainable," sighed Samoilenko. "Only here's what I don't understand. You're a man of the greatest intelligence, explain it to me, please. There are these little beasts, you know, no bigger than a rat, pretty to look at but mean and immoral in the highest degree, let me tell you. Suppose such a beast is walking along through the forest; it sees a little bird, catches it, and eats it up. It goes on and sees a nest with eggs in the grass; it doesn't want any more grub, it's not hungry, but even so, it bites into an egg and throws the others out of the nest with its paw. Then it meets a frog and starts playing with it. It tortures the frog to death, goes on, licking its chops, and meets a beetle. Swats the beetle with its paw... And it ruins and destroys everything in its way... It crawls into other animals' holes, digs up anthills for nothing, cracks open snail shells... It meets a rat and gets into a fight with it; it sees a snake or a mouse and has to strangle it. And this goes on all day. So tell me, what is the need for such a beast? Why was it created?"

"I don't know what beast you're talking about," said von Koren, "probably some insectivore. Well, so what? It caught a bird because the bird was careless; it destroyed the nest of eggs because the bird wasn't skillful, it made the nest poorly and didn't camouflage it. The frog probably had some flaw in its coloring, otherwise it wouldn't have seen it, and so on. Your beast destroys only the weak, the unskilled, the careless—in short, those who have flaws that nature does not find it necessary to transmit to posterity. Only the more nimble, careful, strong, and developed remain alive. Thus your little beast, without suspecting it, serves the great purposes of perfection."

"Yes, yes, yes... By the way, brother," Samoilenko said casually, "how about lending me a hundred roubles?"

"Fine. Among the insectivores, very interesting species occur. For instance, the mole. They say it's useful because it destroys harmful insects. The story goes that a German once sent the emperor Wilhelm I a coat made of moleskins, and that the emperor supposedly reprimanded him for destroying so many of the useful animals. And yet the mole yields nothing to your little beast in cruelty, and is very harmful besides, because it does awful damage to the fields."

Von Koren opened a box and took out a hundred-rouble bill.

"The mole has a strong chest, like the bat," he went on, locking the box, "its bones and muscles are awfully well developed, its jaw is extraordinarily well equipped. If it had the dimensions of an elephant, it would be an all-destructive, invincible animal. It's interesting that when two moles meet underground, they both begin to prepare a flat space, as if by arrangement; they need this space in order to fight more conveniently. Once they've made it, they start a cruel battle and struggle until the weaker one falls. Here, take the hundred roubles," said von Koren, lowering his voice, "but only on condition that you're not taking it for Laevsky."

"And what if it is for Laevsky!" Samoilenko flared up. "Is that any business of yours?"

"I can't give money for Laevsky. I know you like lending. You'd lend to the robber Kerim if he asked you, but, excuse me, in that direction I can't help you."

"Yes, I'm asking for Laevsky!" said Samoilenko, getting up and waving his right arm. "Yes! For Laevsky! And no devil or demon has the right to teach me how I should dispose of my money. You don't want to give it to me? Eh?"

The deacon burst out laughing.

"Don't seethe, but reason," said the zoologist. "To be Mr. Laevsky's benefactor is, in my opinion, as unintelligent as watering weeds or feeding locusts."

"And in my opinion, it's our duty to help our neighbors!" cried Samoilenko.

"In that case, help this hungry Turk who's lying by the hedge! He's a worker and more necessary, more useful than your Laevsky. Give him this hundred roubles! Or donate me a hundred roubles for the expedition!"

"Will you lend it to me or not, I ask you?"

"Tell me frankly: what does he need the money for?"

"It's no secret. He has to go to Petersburg on Saturday."

"So that's it!" von Koren drew out. "Aha . . . We understand. And will she be going with him, or what?"

"She remains here for the time being. He'll settle his affairs in Petersburg and send her money, and then she'll go."

"Clever! . . ." said the zoologist and laughed a brief tenor laugh. "Clever! Smart thinking!"

He quickly went up to Samoilenko and, planting himself face-to-face with him, looking into his eyes, asked:

"Speak frankly to me: he's fallen out of love? Right? Speak: he's fallen out of love? Right?"

"Right," Samoilenko brought out and broke into a sweat.

"How loathsome!" said von Koren, and one could see by his face that he felt loathing. "There are two possibilities, Alexander Davidych: either you're in conspiracy with him or, forgive me, you're a simpleton. Don't you understand that he's taking you in like a little boy, in the most shameful way? It's clear as day that he wants to get rid of her and leave her here. She'll be left on your neck, and it's clear as day that you'll have to send her to Petersburg at your own expense. Has your excellent friend so bedazzled you with his merits that you don't see even the simplest things?"

"Those are nothing but conjectures," said Samoilenko, sitting down.

"Conjectures? And why is he going alone and not with her? And why, ask him, shouldn't she go on ahead and he come later? A sly beast!"

Oppressed by sudden doubts and suspicions concerning his friend, Samoilenko suddenly weakened and lowered his tone.

"But this is impossible!" he said, remembering the night Laevsky had spent at his place. "He suffers so!"

"What of it? Thieves and incendiaries also suffer!"

"Even supposing you're right . . ." Samoilenko said, pondering. "Let's assume . . . But he's a young man, in foreign parts . . . a student, but we've also been students, and except for us, there's nobody to support him."

"To help him in his abomination only because at different points you and he were at the university and both did nothing there! What nonsense!"

"Wait, let's reason with equanimity. It's possible, I suppose, to arrange it like this..." Samoilenko reasoned, twisting his fingers. "You see, I'll give him money, but I'll take from him his gentleman's word of honor that he will send Nadezhda Fyodorovna money for the trip in a week."

"And he'll give you his word of honor, and even shed a tear and believe himself, but what is his word worth? He won't keep it, and when, in a year or two, you meet him on Nevsky Prospect arm in arm with a new love, he'll justify himself by saying civilization has crippled him and he's a chip off Rudin's block.[27] Drop him, for God's sake! Walk away from this muck, and don't rummage in it with both hands!"

Samoilenko thought for a minute and said resolutely:

"But even so, I'll give him the money. As you like. I'm unable to refuse a man on the basis of conjectures alone."

"Excellent. Go and kiss him."

"So give me the hundred roubles," Samoilenko asked timidly.

"I won't."

Silence ensued. Samoilenko went completely weak; his face acquired a guilty, ashamed, and fawning expression, and it was somehow strange to see this pitiful, childishly abashed face on a huge man wearing epaulettes and decorations.

"The local bishop goes around his diocese not in a carriage but on horseback," said the deacon, putting down his pen. "The sight of him riding a little horse is extremely touching. His simplicity and modesty are filled with biblical grandeur."

"Is he a good man?" asked von Koren, who was glad to change the subject.

"But of course. If he wasn't good, how could he have been ordained a bishop?"

"There are some very good and gifted people among the bishops," said von Koren. "Only it's a pity that many of them have the weakness of imagining themselves statesmen. One occupies himself with Russification, another criticizes science. That's not their business. They'd do better to stop by at the consistory more often."

"A worldly man cannot judge a bishop."

"Why not, Deacon? A bishop is the same sort of man as I am."

"The same and not the same," the deacon became offended and again took up his pen. "If you were the same, grace would have rested upon you, and you'd have been a bishop yourself, but since you're not a bishop, it means you're not the same."

"Don't drivel, Deacon!" Samoilenko said in anguish. "Listen, here's what I've come up with," he turned to von Koren. "Don't give me that hundred roubles. You're going to be my boarder for another three months before winter, so give me the money for those three months ahead of time."

"I won't."

Samoilenko blinked and turned purple, mechanically drew the book with the phalangid towards him and looked at it, then got up and took his hat. Von Koren felt sorry for him.

"Just try living and having anything to do with such gentlemen!" said the zoologist, and he kicked some paper into the corner in indignation. "Understand that this is not kindness, not love, but pusillanimity, license, poison! What reason achieves, your flabby, worthless hearts destroy! When I was sick with typhoid as a schoolboy, my aunt, in her compassion, overfed me with pickled mushrooms, and I nearly died. Understand, you and my aunt both, that love for man should not be in your heart, not in the pit of your stomach, not in your lower back, but here!"

Von Koren slapped himself on the forehead.

"Take it!" he said and flung the hundred-rouble bill.

"You needn't be angry, Kolya," Samoilenko said meekly, folding the bill. "I understand you very well, but . . . put yourself in my position."

"You're an old woman, that's what!"

The deacon guffawed.

"Listen, Alexander Davidych, one last request!" von Koren said hotly. "When you give that finagler the money, set him a condition: let him leave together with his lady or send her on ahead, otherwise don't give it. There's no point in being ceremonious with him. Just tell him that, and if you don't, on my word of honor, I'll go to his office and chuck him down the stairs, and you I'll have nothing more to do with. Be it known to you!"

"So? If he goes with her or sends her ahead, it's the more convenient for him," said Samoilenko. "He'll even be glad. Well, good-bye."

He affectionately took his leave and went out, but before closing the door behind him, he turned to look at von Koren, made an awful face, and said:

"It's the Germans that spoiled you, brother! Yes! The Germans!"

XII

THE NEXT DAY, Thursday, Marya Konstantinovna celebrated her Kostya's birthday. At noon everyone was invited for cake, and in the evening for hot chocolate. When Laevsky and Nadezhda Fyodorovna came in the evening, the zoologist, already sitting in the drawing room and drinking chocolate, asked Samoilenko:

"Did you speak to him?"

"Not yet."

"Watch out, don't be ceremonious. I don't understand the impudence of these people! They know very well this family's view of their cohabitation, and yet they keep coming here."

"If you pay attention to every prejudice," said Samoilenko, "you won't be able to go anywhere."

"Is the loathing of the masses for licentiousness and love outside marriage a prejudice?"

"Of course. Prejudice and hatefulness. When soldiers see a girl of light behavior, they guffaw and whistle, but ask them what they are themselves."

"It's not for nothing that they whistle. That sluts strangle their illegitimate children and go to hard labor, and that Anna Karenina threw herself under a train, and that they tar people's gates in the villages, and that you and I, for some unknown reason, like Katya's purity, and that everyone vaguely feels the need for pure love, though he knows that such love doesn't exist—is all that a prejudice? That, brother, is all that's left of natural selection, and if it weren't for this obscure force that regulates relations between the sexes, the Messers Laevsky would show us what o'clock it is, and mankind would turn degenerate in two years."

Laevsky came into the drawing room; he greeted everyone and, shaking von Koren's hand, gave him an ingratiating smile. He waited for an opportune moment and said to Samoilenko:

"Excuse me, Alexander Davidych, I must have a couple of words with you."

Samoilenko got up, put his arm around his waist, and the two went to Nikodim Alexandrych's study.

"Tomorrow is Friday..." said Laevsky, biting his nails. "Did you get what you promised?"

"I got only two hundred and ten. I'll get the rest today or tomorrow. Don't worry."

"Thank God!..." sighed Laevsky, and his hands trembled with joy. "You are saving me, Alexander Davidych, and, I swear to you by God, by my happiness, and by whatever you like, I'll send you this money as soon as I get there. And the old debt as well."

"Look here, Vanya..." said Samoilenko, taking him by a button and blushing. "Excuse me for interfering in your

family affairs, but . . . why don't you take Nadezhda Fyodorovna with you?"

"You odd fellow, how could I? One of us certainly has to
stay, otherwise my creditors will start howling. I owe some
seven hundred roubles in various shops, if not more. Wait,
I'll send them the money, stick it in their teeth, and then she
can leave here."

"Well . . . But why don't you send her on ahead?"

"Ah, my God, how can I?" Laevsky was horrified. "She's
a woman, what will she do there alone? What does she
understand? It would just be a loss of time and an unnecessary
waste of money."

"Reasonable . . ." thought Samoilenko, but he remembered his conversation with von Koren, looked down, and
said sullenly:

"I can't agree with you. Either go with her or send her
on ahead, otherwise . . . otherwise I won't give you the
money. That is my final word . . ."

He backed up, collided with the door, and went out into
the drawing room red-faced, in terrible embarrassment.

"Friday . . . Friday," thought Laevsky, returning to the
drawing room. "Friday . . ."

He was handed a cup of chocolate. He burned his lips and
tongue with the hot chocolate and thought:

"Friday . . . Friday . . ."

For some reason, he could not get the word "Friday" out
of his head; he thought of nothing but Friday, and the only
thing clear to him, not in his head but somewhere under his
heart, was that he was not to leave on Saturday. Before him
stood Nikodim Alexandrych, neat, his hair brushed forward
on his temples, and begging him:

"Eat something, I humbly beg you, sir . . ."

Marya Konstantinovna showed her guests Katya's grades,
saying in a drawn-out manner:

"Nowadays it's terribly, terribly difficult to study! So many requirements . . ."

"Mama!" moaned Katya, not knowing where to hide from embarrassment and praise.

Laevsky also looked at her grades and praised her. Bible studies, Russian, conduct, A's and B's began leaping in his eyes, and all of it, together with the importunate Friday, Nikodim Alexandrych's brushed-up temples, and Katya's red cheeks, stood before him as such boundless, invincible boredom that he almost cried out in despair and asked himself: "Can it be, can it be that I won't leave?"

They set two card tables next to each other and sat down to play postman's knock. Laevsky also sat down.

"Friday . . . Friday . . ." he thought, smiling and taking a pencil from his pocket. "Friday . . ."

He wanted to think over his situation and was afraid to think. It frightened him to admit that the doctor had caught him in the deception he had so long and so thoroughly concealed from himself. Each time he thought of his future, he did not give free rein to his thoughts. He would get on the train and go—that solved the problem of his life, and he did not let his thoughts go any further. Like a faint, far-off light in a field, from time to time the thought glimmered in his head that somewhere, in one of Petersburg's lanes, in the distant future, in order to break with Nadezhda Fyodorovna and pay his debts, he would have to resort to a small lie. He would lie only once, and then a complete renewal would come. And that was good: at the cost of a small lie, he would buy a big truth.

Now, though, when the doctor crudely hinted at the deceit by his refusal, it became clear to him that he would need the lie not only in the distant future but today, and tomorrow, and in a month, and maybe even to the end of his life. Indeed, in order to leave, he would have to lie to Nadezhda Fyodorovna, his creditors, and his superiors; then, in order to get money in Petersburg, he would have to lie to his mother and tell her he had already broken with Nadezhda Fyodorovna; and his mother would not give him more than five hundred roubles—meaning that he had already deceived the doctor, because he would not be able to send him the money soon. Then, when Nadezhda Fyodorovna came to Petersburg, he would have to resort to a whole series of small and large deceptions in order to break with her; and again there would be tears, boredom, a hateful life, remorse, and thus no renewal at all. Deception and nothing more. A whole mountain of lies grew in Laevsky's imagination. To leap over it at one jump, and not lie piecemeal, he would have to resolve upon a stiff measure—for instance, without saying a word, to get up from his place, put on his hat, and leave straightaway without money, without a word said, but Laevsky felt that this was impossible for him.

"Friday, Friday . . ." he thought. "Friday . . ."

They wrote notes, folded them in two, and put them in Nikodim Alexandrych's old top hat, and when enough notes had accumulated, Kostya, acting as postman, went around the table handing them out. The deacon, Katya, and Kostya, who received funny notes and tried to write something funny, were delighted.

"We must have a talk," Nadezhda Fyodorovna read in her note. She exchanged glances with Marya Konstantinovna, who gave her almond-butter smile and nodded her head.

"What is there to talk about?" thought Nadezhda Fyodorovna. "If it's impossible to tell everything, there's no point in talking."

Before going to the party, she had tied Laevsky's necktie, and this trifling thing had filled her soul with tenderness and sorrow. The anxiety on his face, his absentminded gazes, his paleness, and the incomprehensible change that had come over him lately, and the fact that she was keeping a terrible, repulsive secret from him, and that her hands had trembled as she tied his necktie—all this, for some reason, told her that they would not be living together for long. She gazed at him as at an icon, with fear and repentance, and thought: "Forgive me, forgive me . . ." Atchmianov sat across the table from her and did not tear his black, amorous eyes from her; desires stirred her, she was ashamed of herself and feared that even anguish and sorrow would not keep her from yielding to the impure passion, if not today, then tomorrow, and that, like a drunkard on a binge, she was no longer able to stop.

So as not to prolong this life, which was disgraceful for her and insulting to Laevsky, she decided to leave. She would tearfully implore him to let her go, and if he objected, she would leave him secretly. She would not tell him what had happened. Let him preserve a pure memory of her.

"Love you, love you, love you," she read. This was from Atchmianov.

She would live somewhere in a remote place, work, and send Laevsky, "from an unknown person," money, embroidered shirts, tobacco, and go back to him only in his old age or in case he became dangerously ill and needed a sick nurse. When, in his old age, he learned the reasons why she had refused to be his wife and had left him, he would appreciate her sacrifice and forgive her.

"You have a long nose." That must be from the deacon or from Kostya.

Nadezhda Fyodorovna imagined how, in saying good-bye to Laevsky, she would hug him tight, kiss his hand, and swear to love him all, all her life, and later, living in a remote place, among strangers, she would think every day that she had a friend somewhere, a beloved man, pure, noble, and lofty, who preserved a pure memory of her.

"If tonight you don't arrange to meet me, I shall take measures, I assure you on my word of honor. One does not treat decent people this way, you must understand that." This was from Kirilin.

XIII

LAEVSKY RECEIVED TWO NOTES; he unfolded one and read: "Don't go away, my dear heart."

"Who could have written that?" he wondered. "Not Samoilenko, of course... And not the deacon, since he doesn't know I want to leave. Von Koren, maybe?"

The zoologist was bent over the table, drawing a pyramid. It seemed to Laevsky that his eyes were smiling.

"Samoilenko probably blabbed..." thought Laevsky.

The other note, written in the same affected handwriting, with long tails and flourishes, read: "Somebody's not leaving on Saturday."

"Stupid jeering," thought Laevsky. "Friday, Friday..."

Something rose in his throat. He touched his collar and coughed, but instead of coughing, laughter burst from his throat.

"Ha, ha, ha!" he guffawed. "Ha, ha, ha!" ("Why am I doing this?" he wondered.) "Ha, ha, ha!"

He tried to control himself, covered his mouth with his hand, but his chest and neck were choking with laughter, and his hand could not cover his mouth.

"How stupid this is, though!" he thought, rocking with laughter. "Have I lost my mind, or what?"

His laughter rose higher and higher and turned into something like a lapdog's yelping. Laevsky wanted to get up from the table, but his legs would not obey him, and his right hand somehow strangely, against his will, leaped across the table, convulsively catching at pieces of paper and clutching them. He saw astonished looks, the serious, frightened face of Samoilenko, and the zoologist's gaze, full of cold mockery and squeamishness, and realized that he was having hysterics.

"How grotesque, how shameful," he thought, feeling the

warmth of tears on his face. "Ah, ah, what shame! This has never happened to me before . . ."

Then they took him under the arms and, supporting his head from behind, led him somewhere; then a glass gleamed in front of his eyes and knocked against his teeth, and water spilled on his chest; then there was a small room, two beds side by side in the middle, covered with snow-white bedspreads. He collapsed onto one of the beds and broke into sobs.

"Never mind, never mind . . ." Samoilenko was saying. "It happens . . . It happens . . ."

Cold with fear, trembling all over, and anticipating something terrible, Nadezhda Fyodorovna stood by the bed, asking:

"What's wrong with you? What is it? For God's sake, speak . . ."

"Can Kirilin have written him something?" she wondered.

"Never mind . . ." said Laevsky, laughing and crying. "Go away . . . my dove."

His face expressed neither hatred nor revulsion: that meant he knew nothing. Nadezhda Fyodorovna calmed down a little and went to the drawing room.

"Don't worry, dear!" Marya Konstantinovna said, sitting down beside her and taking her hand. "It will pass. Men are as weak as we sinners. The two of you are living through a crisis now . . . it's so understandable! Well, dear, I'm waiting for an answer. Let's talk."

"No, let's not . . ." said Nadezhda Fyodorovna, listening to Laevsky's sobbing. "I'm in anguish . . . Allow me to leave."

"Ah, my dear, my dear!" Marya Konstantinovna was alarmed. "Do you think I'll let you go without supper? We'll have a bite, and then you're free to leave."

"I'm in anguish . . ." whispered Nadezhda Fyodorovna, and to keep from falling, she gripped the armrest of the chair with both hands.

"He's in convulsions!" von Koren said gaily, coming into the drawing room, but, seeing Nadezhda Fyodorovna, he became embarrassed and left.

When the hysterics were over, Laevsky sat on the strange bed and thought:

"Disgrace, I howled like a little girl! I must be ridiculous and vile. I'll leave by the back stairs ... Though that would mean I attach serious significance to my hysterics. I ought to downplay them like a joke ... "

He looked in the mirror, sat for a little while, and went to the drawing room.

"Here I am!" he said, smiling; he was painfully ashamed, and he felt that the others were also ashamed in his presence. "Imagine that," he said, taking a seat. "I was sitting there and suddenly, you know, I felt an awful, stabbing pain in my side ... unbearable, my nerves couldn't stand it, and ... and this stupid thing occurred. This nervous age of ours, there's nothing to be done!"

Over supper he drank wine, talked, and from time to time, sighing spasmodically, stroked his side as if to show that the pain could still be felt. And nobody except Nadezhda Fyodorovna believed him, and he saw it.

After nine o'clock they went for a stroll on the boulevard. Nadezhda Fyodorovna, fearing that Kirilin might start talking to her, tried to keep near Marya Konstantinovna and the children all the time. She grew weak from fright and anguish and, anticipating a fever, suffered and could barely move her legs, but she would not go home, because she was sure that either Kirilin or Atchmianov, or both of them, would follow her. Kirilin walked behind her, next to Nikodim Alexandrych, and intoned in a low voice:

"I will not alo-o-ow myself to be to-o-oyed with! I will not alo-o-ow it!"

From the boulevard they turned towards the pavilion, and

for a long time gazed at the phosphorescent sea. Von Koren began to explain what made it phosphoresce.

XIV

"HOWEVER, IT'S TIME for my vint... They're waiting for me," said Laevsky. "Good night, ladies and gentlemen."

"Wait, I'll go with you," said Nadezhda Fyodorovna, and she took his arm. They took leave of the company and walked off. Kirilin also took his leave, said he was going the same way, and walked with them.

"What will be, will be..." thought Nadezhda Fyodorovna. "Let it come..."

It seemed to her that all her bad memories had left her head and were walking in the darkness beside her and breathing heavily, while she herself, like a fly that had fallen into ink, forced herself to crawl down the sidewalk, staining Laevsky's side and arm with black. If Kirilin does something bad, she thought, it will not be his fault, but hers alone. There was a time when no man would have talked to her as Kirilin had done, and she herself had snapped off that time like a thread and destroyed it irretrievably—whose fault was that? Intoxicated by her own desires, she had begun to smile at a totally unknown man, probably only because he was stately and tall, after two meetings she had become bored with him and had dropped him, and didn't that, she now thought, give him the right to act as he pleased with her?

"Here, my dove, I'll say good-bye to you," said Laevsky, stopping. "Ilya Mikhailych will see you home."

He bowed to Kirilin and quickly headed across the boulevard, went down the street to Sheshkovsky's house, where there were lights in the windows, and then they heard the gate slam.

"Allow me to explain myself to you," Kirilin began. "I'm

not a boy, not some sort of Atchkasov, or Latchkasov, or Zatchkasov . . . I demand serious attention!"

Nadezhda Fyodorovna's heart was beating fast. She made no reply.

"At first I explained the abrupt change in your behavior towards me by coquetry," Kirilin went on, "but now I see that you simply do not know how to behave with respectable people. You simply wanted to toy with me as with this Armenian boy, but I am a respectable person, and I demand to be treated as a respectable person. And so I am at your service . . ."

"I'm in anguish . . ." said Nadezhda Fyodorovna, and she turned away to hide her tears.

"I am also in anguish, but what follows from that?"

Kirilin was silent for a while and then said distinctly, measuredly:

"I repeat, madam, that if you do not grant me a meeting tonight, then tonight I shall make a scandal."

"Let me go tonight," said Nadezhda Fyodorovna, and she did not recognize her own voice, so pathetic and thin it was.

"I must teach you a lesson . . . Forgive me this rude tone, but it's necessary for me to teach you a lesson. Yes, ma'am, unfortunately I must teach you a lesson. I demand two meetings: tonight and tomorrow. After tomorrow you are completely free and can go wherever you like with whomever you like. Tonight and tomorrow."

Nadezhda Fyodorovna went up to her gate and stopped.

"Let me go!" she whispered, trembling all over and seeing nothing before her in the darkness except a white tunic. "You're right, I'm a terrible woman . . . I'm to blame, but let me go . . . I beg you . . ." she touched his cold hand and shuddered, "I implore you . . ."

"Alas!" sighed Kirilin. "Alas! It is not in my plans to let you go, I merely want to teach you a lesson, to make you understand, and besides, madam, I have very little faith in women."

"I'm in anguish..."

Nadezhda Fyodorovna listened to the steady sound of the sea, looked at the sky strewn with stars, and wished she could end it all quickly and be rid of this cursed sensation of life with its sea, stars, men, fever...

"Only not in my house..." she said coldly. "Take me somewhere."

"Let's go to Miuridov's. That's best."

"Where is it?"

"By the old ramparts."

She walked quickly down the street and then turned into a lane that led to the mountains. It was dark. On the pavement here and there lay pale strips of light from lighted windows, and it seemed to her that she was like a fly that first fell into ink, then crawled out again into the light. Kirilin walked behind her. At one point he stumbled, nearly fell, and laughed.

"He's drunk..." thought Nadezhda Fyodorovna. "It's all the same... all the same... Let it be."

Atchmianov also soon took leave of the company and followed Nadezhda Fyodorovna so as to invite her for a boat ride. He went up to her house and looked across the front garden: the windows were wide open, there was no light.

"Nadezhda Fyodorovna!" he called.

A minute passed. He called again.

"Who's there?" came Olga's voice.

"Is Nadezhda Fyodorovna at home?"

"No. She hasn't come yet."

"Strange... Very strange," thought Atchmianov, beginning to feel greatly worried. "She did go home..."

He strolled along the boulevard, then down the street, and looked in Sheshkovsky's windows. Laevsky, without his frock coat, was sitting at the table and looking intently at his cards.

"Strange, strange..." murmured Atchmianov, and, recollecting the hysterics that had come over Laevsky, he felt ashamed. "If she's not at home, where is she?"

And again he went to Nadezhda Fyodorovna's apartment and looked at the dark windows.

"Deceit, deceit..." he thought, remembering that she herself, on meeting him that noon at the Bitiugovs', had promised to go for a boat ride with him in the evening.

The windows of the house where Kirilin lived were dark, and a policeman sat asleep on a bench by the gate. As he looked at the windows and the policeman, everything became clear to Atchmianov. He decided to go home and went, but again wound up by Nadezhda Fyodorovna's. There he sat down on a bench and took off his hat, feeling his head burning with jealousy and offense.

The clock on the town church struck only twice a day, at noon and at midnight. Soon after it struck midnight, he heard hurrying footsteps.

"So, tomorrow evening at Miuridov's again!" Atchmianov heard, and recognized Kirilin's voice. "At eight o'clock. Good-bye, ma'am!"

Nadezhda Fyodorovna appeared by the front garden. Not noticing Atchmianov sitting on the bench, she walked past him like a shadow, opened the gate, and, leaving it open, walked into the house. In her room, she lighted a candle, undressed quickly, yet did not go to bed, but sank onto her knees in front of a chair, put her arms around it, and leaned her forehead against it.

Laevsky came home past two o'clock.

XV

HAVING DECIDED NOT to lie all at once, but piecemeal, Laevsky went to Samoilenko the next day after one o'clock to ask for the money, so as to be sure to leave on Saturday. After yesterday's hysterics, which to the painful state of his mind had added an acute sense of shame, remaining in town

83

was unthinkable. If Samoilenko insists on his conditions, he thought, he could agree to them and take the money, and tomorrow, just at the time of departure, tell him that Nadezhda Fyodorovna had refused to go; he could persuade her in the evening that the whole thing was being done for her benefit. And if Samoilenko, who was obviously under the influence of von Koren, refused entirely or suggested some new conditions, then he, Laevsky, would leave that same day on a freighter or even a sailboat, for Novy Afon or Novorossiisk, send his mother a humiliating telegram from there, and live there until his mother sent him money for the trip.

Coming to Samoilenko's, he found von Koren in the drawing room. The zoologist had just come for dinner and, as usual, had opened the album and was studying the men in top hats and women in caps.

"How inopportune," thought Laevsky, seeing him. "He may hinder everything."

"Good afternoon!"

"Good afternoon," replied von Koren without looking at him.

"Is Alexander Davidych at home?"

"Yes. In the kitchen."

Laevsky went to the kitchen, but, seeing through the doorway that Samoilenko was busy with the salad, he returned to the drawing room and sat down. He always felt awkward in the zoologist's presence, and now he was afraid he would have to talk about his hysterics. More than a minute passed in silence. Von Koren suddenly raised his eyes to Laevsky and asked:

"How do you feel after yesterday?"

"Splendid," Laevsky replied, blushing. "Essentially there was nothing very special . . ."

"Until last night I assumed that only ladies had hysterics, and so I thought at first that what you had was Saint Vitus's dance."

Laevsky smiled ingratiatingly and thought:

"How indelicate on his part. He knows perfectly well that it's painful for me..."

"Yes, it was a funny story," he said, still smiling. "I spent this whole morning laughing. The curious thing about a fit of hysterics is that you know it's absurd, and you laugh at it in your heart, and at the same time you're sobbing. In our nervous age, we're slaves to our nerves; they're our masters and do whatever they like with us. In this respect, civilization is a dubious blessing..."

Laevsky talked, and found it unpleasant that von Koren listened to him seriously and attentively, and looked at him attentively, without blinking, as if studying him; and he felt vexed with himself for being unable, despite all his dislike of von Koren, to drive the ingratiating smile from his face.

"Though I must confess," he went on, "there were more immediate causes of the fit, and rather substantial ones. My health has been badly shaken lately. Add to that the boredom, the constant lack of money... the lack of people and common interests... My situation's worse than a governor's."

"Yes, your situation's hopeless," said von Koren.

These calm, cold words, containing either mockery or an uninvited prophecy, offended Laevsky. He remembered the zoologist's gaze yesterday, full of mockery and squeamishness, paused briefly, and asked, no longer smiling:

"And how are you informed of my situation?"

"You've just been talking about it yourself, and your friends take such a warm interest in you that one hears of nothing but you all day long."

"What friends? Samoilenko, is it?"

"Yes, him, too."

"I'd ask Alexander Davidych and my friends generally to be less concerned about me."

"Here comes Samoilenko, ask him to be less concerned about you."

"I don't understand your tone . . ." Laevsky murmured; he was gripped by such a feeling as though he had only now understood that the zoologist hated him, despised and jeered at him, and that the zoologist was his worst and most implacable enemy. "Save that tone for somebody else," he said softly, unable to speak loudly from the hatred that was already tightening around his chest and neck, as the desire to laugh had done yesterday.

Samoilenko came in without his frock coat, sweaty and crimson from the stuffiness of the kitchen.

"Ah, you're here?" he said. "Greetings, dear heart. Have you had dinner? Don't be ceremonious, tell me: have you had dinner?"

"Alexander Davidych," said Laevsky, getting up, "if I turned to you with an intimate request, it did not mean I was releasing you from the obligation of being modest and respecting other people's secrets."

"What's wrong?" Samoilenko was surprised.

"If you don't have the money," Laevsky went on, raising his voice and shifting from one foot to the other in agitation, "then don't give it to me, refuse, but why announce on every street corner that my situation is hopeless and all that? I cannot bear these benefactions and friendly services when one does a kopeck's worth with a rouble's worth of talk! You may boast of your benefactions as much as you like, but no one gave you the right to reveal my secrets!"

"What secrets?" asked Samoilenko, perplexed and beginning to get angry. "If you came to abuse me, go away. You can come later!"

He remembered the rule that, when angry with your neighbor, you should mentally start counting to a hundred and calm down; and he started counting quickly.

"I beg you not to be concerned about me!" Laevsky went on. "Don't pay attention to me. And who has any business with me and how I live? Yes, I want to go away! Yes, I run up debts, drink, live with another man's wife, I'm hysterical, I'm banal, I'm not as profound as some are, but whose business is that? Respect the person!"

"Excuse me, brother," said Samoilenko, having counted up to thirty-five, "but..."

"Respect the person!" Laevsky interrupted him. "This constant talk on another man's account, the ohs and ahs, the constant sniffing out, the eavesdropping, these friendly commiserations... devil take it! They lend me money and set conditions as if I was a little boy! I'm treated like the devil knows what! I don't want anything!" cried Laevsky, reeling with agitation and fearing he might have hysterics again. "So I won't leave on Saturday," flashed through his mind. "I don't want anything! I only beg you, please, to deliver me from your care! I'm not a little boy and not a madman, and I beg you to relieve me of this supervision!"

The deacon came in and, seeing Laevsky, pale, waving his arms, and addressing his strange speech to the portrait of Prince Vorontsov, stopped by the door as if rooted to the spot.

"This constant peering into my soul," Laevsky went on, "offends my human dignity, and I beg the volunteer detectives to stop their spying! Enough!"

"What... what did you say, sir?" asked Samoilenko, having counted to a hundred, turning purple, and going up to Laevsky.

"Enough!" said Laevsky, gasping and taking his cap.

"I am a Russian doctor, a nobleman, and a state councillor!" Samoilenko said measuredly. "I have never been a spy, and I will not allow anyone to insult me!" he said in a cracked voice, emphasizing the last words. "Silence!"

The deacon, who had never seen the doctor so majestic, puffed up, crimson, and fearsome, covered his mouth, ran out to the front room, and there rocked with laughter. As if through a fog, Laevsky saw von Koren get up and, putting his hands in his trouser pockets, stand in that pose as if waiting for what would happen next. Laevsky found this relaxed pose insolent and offensive in the highest degree.

"Kindly take back your words!" cried Samoilenko.

Laevsky, who no longer remembered what words he had spoken, answered:

"Leave me alone! I don't want anything! All I want is that you and these Germans of Yid extraction leave me alone! Otherwise I'll take measures! I'll fight!"

"Now I see," said von Koren, stepping away from the table. "Mr. Laevsky wants to divert himself with a duel before his departure. I can give him that satisfaction. Mr. Laevsky, I accept your challenge."

"My challenge?" Laevsky said softly, going up to the zoologist and looking with hatred at his swarthy forehead and curly hair. "My challenge? If you please! I hate you! Hate you!"

"Very glad. Tomorrow morning early, by Kerbalai's, with all the details to your taste. And now get out of here."

"I hate you!" Laevsky said softly, breathing heavily. "I've hated you for a long time! A duel! Yes!"

"Take him away, Alexander Davidych, or else I'll leave," said von Koren. "He's going to bite me."

Von Koren's calm tone cooled the doctor down; he somehow suddenly came to himself, recovered his senses, put his arm around Laevsky's waist, and, leading him away from the zoologist, mumured in a gentle voice, trembling with agitation:

"My friends . . . good, kind friends . . . You got excited, but that will do . . . that will do . . . My friends . . ."

Hearing his soft, friendly voice, Laevsky felt that something unprecedented and monstrous had just taken place in his life, as if he had nearly been run over by a train; he almost burst into tears, waved his hand, and rushed from the room.

"To experience another man's hatred of you, to show yourself in the most pathetic, despicable, helpless way before the man who hates you—my God, how painful it is!" he thought shortly afterwards, sitting in the pavilion and feeling something like rust on his body from the just experienced hatred of another man. "How crude it is, my God!"

Cold water with cognac cheered him up. He clearly pictured von Koren's calm, haughty face, his gaze yesterday, his carpetlike shirt, his voice, his white hands, and a heavy hatred, passionate and hungry, stirred in his breast and demanded satisfaction. In his mind, he threw von Koren to the ground and started trampling him with his feet. He recalled everything that had happened in the minutest detail, and wondered how he could smile ingratiatingly at a nonentity and generally value the opinion of petty little people, unknown to anyone, who lived in a worthless town which, it seemed, was not even on the map and which not a single decent person in Petersburg knew about. If this wretched little town were suddenly to fall through the earth or burn down, people in Russia would read the telegram about it with the same boredom as the announcement of a sale of secondhand furniture. To kill von Koren tomorrow or leave him alive was in any case equally useless and uninteresting. To shoot him in the leg or arm, to wound him, then laugh at him, and, as an insect with a torn-off leg gets lost in the grass, so let him with his dull suffering lose himself afterwards in a crowd of the same nonentities as himself.

Laevsky went to Sheshkovsky, told him about it all, and invited him to be his second; then they both went to the head of the post and telegraph office, invited him to be a second as well, and stayed with him for dinner. At dinner they joked and laughed a great deal; Laevsky made fun of the fact that he barely knew how to shoot, and called himself a royal marksman and a Wilhelm Tell.

"This gentleman must be taught a lesson..." he kept saying.

After dinner they sat down to play cards. Laevsky played,

drank wine, and thought how generally stupid and senseless dueling was, because it did not solve the problem but only complicated it, but that sometimes one could not do without it. For instance, in the present case, he could not plead about von Koren before the justice of the peace! And the impending duel was also good in that, after it, he would no longer be able to stay in town. He became slightly drunk, diverted himself with cards, and felt good.

But when the sun set and it grew dark, uneasiness came over him. It was not the fear of death, because all the while he was having dinner and playing cards, the conviction sat in him, for some reason, that the duel would end in nothing; it was a fear of something unknown, which was to take place tomorrow morning for the first time in his life, and a fear of the coming night . . . He knew that the night would be long, sleepless, and that he would have to think not only about von Koren and his hatred but about that mountain of lies he would have to pass through and which he had neither the strength nor the ability to avoid. It looked as though he had unexpectedly fallen ill; he suddenly lost all interest in cards and people, began fussing, and asked to be allowed to go home. He wanted to go to bed quickly, lie still, and prepare his thoughts for the night. Sheshkovsky and the postal official saw him off and went to von Koren to talk about the duel.

Near his apartment, Laevsky met Atchmianov. The young man was breathless and agitated.

"I've been looking for you, Ivan Andreich!" he said. "I beg you, let's go quickly . . ."

"Where?"

"A gentleman you don't know wishes to see you on very important business. He earnestly requests that you come for a moment. He needs to talk to you about something . . . For him it's the same as life and death . . ."

In his excitement, Atchmianov uttered this with a strong Armenian accent, so that it came out not "life" but "lafe."

"Who is he?" asked Laevsky.

"He asked me not to give his name."

"Tell him I'm busy. Tomorrow, if he likes..."

"Impossible!" Atchmianov became frightened. "He wishes to tell you something very important for you... very important! If you don't go, there will be a disaster."

"Strange..." murmured Laevsky, not understanding why Atchmianov was so agitated and what mysteries there could be in this boring, useless little town. "Strange," he repeated, pondering. "However, let's go. It makes no difference."

Atchmianov quickly went ahead, and he followed. They walked down the street, then into a lane.

"How boring this is," said Laevsky.

"One moment, one moment... It's close by."

Near the old ramparts they took a narrow lane between two fenced lots, then entered some big yard and made for a little house.

"That's Miuridov's house, isn't it?" asked Laevsky.

"Yes."

"But why we came through the back alleys, I don't understand. We could have taken the street. It's closer."

"Never mind, never mind..."

Laevsky also found it strange that Atchmianov led him to the back door and waved his hand as if asking him to walk softly and keep silent.

"This way, this way..." said Atchmianov, cautiously opening the door and going into the hallway on tiptoe. "Quiet, quiet, I beg you... They may hear you."

He listened, drew a deep breath, and said in a whisper:

"Open this door and go in... Don't be afraid."

Laevsky, perplexed, opened the door and went into a room with a low ceiling and curtained windows. A candle stood on the table.

"Whom do you want?" someone asked in the next room. "Is that you, Miuridka?"

Laevsky turned to that room and saw Kirilin, and beside him Nadezhda Fyodorovna.

He did not hear what was said to him, backed his way out, and did not notice how he ended up in the street. The hatred of von Koren, and the uneasiness—all of it vanished from his soul. Going home, he awkwardly swung his right arm and looked intently under his feet, trying to walk where it was even. At home, in his study, he paced up and down, rubbing his hands and making angular movements with his shoulders and neck, as though his jacket and shirt were too tight for him, then lighted a candle and sat down at the table . . .

XVI

"THE HUMANE SCIENCES, of which you speak, will only satisfy human thought when, in their movement, they meet the exact sciences and go on alongside them. Whether they will meet under a microscope, or in the soliloquies of a new Hamlet, or in a new religion, I don't know, but I think that the earth will be covered with an icy crust before that happens. The most staunch and vital of all humanitarian doctrines is, of course, the teaching of Christ, but look at how differently people understand even that! Some teach us to love all our neighbors, but at the same time make an exception for soldiers, criminals, and madmen: the first they allow to be killed in war, the second to be isolated or executed, and the third they forbid to marry. Other interpreters teach the love of all our neighbors without exception, without distinguishing between pluses and minuses. According to their teaching, if a consumptive or a murderer or an epileptic comes to you and wants to marry your daughter—give her to him; if cretins declare war on the physically and mentally healthy—offer your heads. This preaching of love for love's sake, like art for art's sake, if it could come to power, in the end would lead mankind to total extinction, and thus the most grandiose villainy of all that have ever been done on earth would be accomplished. There are a great many interpretations, and if there are many, then serious thought cannot be satisfied by any one of them, and to the mass of all interpretations hastens to add its own. Therefore never put the question, as you say, on philosophical or so-called Christian grounds; by doing so, you merely get further away from solving it."

The deacon listened attentively to the zoologist, pondered, and asked:

"Was the moral law, which is proper to each and every person, invented by philosophers, or did God create it along with the body?"

"I don't know. But this law is common to all peoples and epochs to such a degree that it seems to me it ought to be acknowledged as organically connected with man. It hasn't been invented, but is and will be. I won't tell you that it will one day be seen under a microscope, but its organic connection is proved by the evidence: serious afflictions of the brain and all so-called mental illnesses, as far as I know, express themselves first of all in a perversion of the moral law."

"Very well, sir. Meaning that, as the stomach wants to eat, so the moral sense wants us to love our neighbor. Right? But our nature, being selfish, resists the voice of conscience and reason, and therefore many brain-racking questions arise. To whom should we turn for the solution of these questions, if you tell me not to put them on philosophical grounds?"

"Turn to the little precise knowledge we have. Trust the evidence and the logic of facts. True, it's scanty, but then it's not as flimsy and diffuse as philosophy. Let's say the moral law demands that you love people. What, then? Love should consist in renouncing everything that harms people in one way or another and threatens them with danger in the present and the future. Our knowledge and the evidence tell you that mankind is threatened by danger on the part of the morally and physically abnormal. If so, then fight with the abnormal. If you're unable to raise them to the norm, you should have enough strength and skill to render them harmless, that is, destroy them."

"So love consists in the strong overcoming the weak."

"Undoubtedly."

"But it was the strong who crucified our Lord Jesus Christ!" the deacon said hotly.

"The point is precisely that it was not the strong who crucified Him but the weak. Human culture has weakened and strives to nullify the struggle for existence and natural selection; hence the rapid proliferation of the weak and their predominance over the strong. Imagine that you manage to instill humane ideas, in an undeveloped, rudimentary form, into bees. What would come of it? The drones, which must be killed, would remain alive, would eat the honey, would corrupt and stifle the bees—the result being that the weak would prevail over the strong, and the latter would degenerate. The same is now happening with mankind: the weak oppress the strong. Among savages, still untouched by culture, the strongest, the wisest, and the most moral goes to the front; he is the leader and master. While we, the cultured, crucified Christ and go on crucifying Him. It means we lack something...And we must restore that 'something' in ourselves, otherwise there will be no end to these misunderstandings."

"But what is your criterion for distinguishing between the strong and the weak?"

"Knowledge and evidence. The consumptive and the scrofulous are recognized by their ailments, and the immoral and mad by their acts."

"But mistakes are possible!"

"Yes, but there's no use worrying about getting your feet wet when there's the threat of a flood."

"That's philosophy," laughed the deacon.

"Not in the least. You're so spoiled by your seminary philosophy that you want to see nothing but fog in everything. The abstract science your young head is stuffed with is called abstract because it abstracts your mind from the evidence. Look the devil straight in the eye, and if he is the devil, say so, and don't go to Kant or Hegel for explanations."

The zoologist paused and went on:

"Two times two is four, and a stone is a stone. Tomorrow we've got a duel. You and I are going to say it's stupid and absurd, that dueling has outlived its time, that an aristocratic duel is essentially no different from a drunken brawl in a pot-house, and even so, we won't stop, we'll go and fight. There is, therefore, a power that is stronger than our reasonings. We shout that war is banditry, barbarism, horror, fratricide, we cannot look at blood without fainting; but the French or the Germans need only insult us and we at once feel a surge of inspiration, we most sincerely shout 'hurrah' and fall upon the enemy, you will call for God's blessing on our weapons, and our valor will evoke universal, and withal sincere, rapture. So again, there is a power that is if not higher, then stronger, than us and our philosophy. We can no more stop it than we can stop this storm cloud moving in from over the sea. Don't be a hypocrite, then, don't show it a fig in the pocket, and don't say: 'Ah, how stupid! Ah, how outdated! Ah, it doesn't agree with the Scriptures!' but look it straight in the eye, acknowledge its reasonable legitimacy, and when it wants, for instance, to destroy the feeble, scrofulous, depraved tribe, don't hinder it with your pills and quotations from the poorly understood Gospel. In Leskov there's a conscientious Danila,[28] who finds a leper outside of town and feeds him and keeps him warm in the name of love and Christ. If this Danila indeed loved people, he would have dragged the leper further away from the town and thrown him into a ditch, and would have gone himself and served the healthy. Christ, I hope, gave us the commandment of reasonable, sensible, and useful love."

"What a one you are!" laughed the deacon. "You don't believe in Christ, so why do you mention Him so often?"

"No, I do believe. Only in my own way, of course, not in yours. Ah, Deacon, Deacon!" the zoologist laughed; he put his arm around the deacon's waist and said gaily: "Well, what then? Shall we go to the duel tomorrow?"

"My dignity doesn't permit it, otherwise I would."

"And what does that mean—'dignity'?"

"I've been ordained. Grace is upon me."

"Ah, Deacon, Deacon," von Koren repeated, laughing. "I love talking with you."

"You say you have faith," said the deacon. "What kind of faith is it? I have an uncle, a priest, who is such a believer that, if there's a drought and he goes to the fields to ask for rain, he takes an umbrella and a leather coat so that he won't get wet on the way back. That's faith! When he talks about Christ, he gives off a glow, and all the peasants burst into sobs. He could stop this storm cloud and put all your powers to flight. Yes . . . faith moves mountains."

The deacon laughed and patted the zoologist on the shoulder.

"So there . . ." he went on. "You keep teaching, you fathom the depths of the sea, you sort out the weak and the strong, you write books and challenge to duels—and everything stays where it was; but watch out, let some feeble little elder babble one little word by the Holy Spirit, or a new Mohammed with a scimitar come riding out of Arabia on a stallion, and everything of yours will go flying topsy-turvy, and in Europe there will be no stone left upon stone."

"Well, Deacon, that's written in the sky with a pitchfork!"

"Faith without works is dead, but works without faith are worse still,[29] merely a waste of time and nothing more."

The doctor appeared on the embankment. He saw the deacon and the zoologist and went up to them.

"Everything seems to be ready," he said, out of breath. "Govorovsky and Boiko will be the seconds. They'll call at five o'clock in the morning. It's really piling up!" he said, looking at the sky. "Can't see a thing! It'll rain soon."

"You'll come with us, I hope?" asked von Koren.

"No, God forbid, I'm worn out as it is. Ustimovich will come in my place. I've already talked with him."

Far across the sea, lightning flashed, and there was a muffled roll of thunder.

"How stifling it is before a storm!" said von Koren. "I'll bet you've already been to Laevsky's and wept on his bosom."

"Why should I go to him?" the doctor said, embarrassed. "What an idea!"

Before sunset he had walked several times up and down the boulevard and the street, hoping to meet Laevsky. He was ashamed of his outburst and of the sudden kindly impulse that had followed the outburst. He wanted to apologize to Laevsky in jocular tones, to chide him, to placate him, and tell him that dueling was a leftover of medieval barbarism, but that providence itself had pointed them to a duel as a means of reconciliation: tomorrow the two of them, most excellent people, of the greatest intelligence, would exchange shots, appreciate each other's nobility, and become friends. But he never once met Laevsky.

"Why should I go to him?" Samoilenko repeated. "I didn't offend him, he offended me. Tell me, for mercy's sake, why did he fall upon me? Did I do anything bad to him? I come into the drawing room and suddenly, for no reason:

spy! Take that! Tell me, how did it start between you? What did you tell him?"

"I told him that his situation was hopeless. And I was right. Only honest people and crooks can find a way out of any situation, but somebody who wants to be an honest man and a crook at the same time has no way out. However, it's already eleven o'clock, gentlemen, and we have to get up early tomorrow."

There was a sudden gust of wind; it raised the dust on the embankment, whirled it around, roared, and drowned out the sound of the sea.

"A squall!" said the deacon. "We must go, we're getting dust in our eyes."

As they left, Samoilenko sighed and said, holding on to his cap:

"Most likely I won't sleep tonight."

"Don't worry," the zoologist laughed. "You can rest easy, the duel will end in nothing. Laevsky will magnanimously fire into the air, he can't do anything else, and most likely I won't fire at all. Ending up in court on account of Laevsky, losing time—the game's not worth the candle. By the way, what's the legal responsibility for dueling?"

"Arrest, and in case of the adversary's death, imprisonment in the fortress for up to three years."

"The Peter-and-Paul fortress?"[30]

"No, a military one, I think."

"I ought to teach that fellow a lesson, though!"

Behind them, lightning flashed over the sea and momentarily lit up the rooftops and mountains. Near the boulevard, the friends went different ways. As the doctor disappeared into the darkness and his footsteps were already dying away, von Koren shouted to him:

"The weather may hinder us tomorrow!"

"It may well! And God grant it!"

"Good night!"

"What—night? What did you say?"

It was hard to hear because of the noise of the wind and the sea and the rolling thunder.

"Never mind!" shouted the zoologist, and he hurried home.

XVII

... in my mind, oppressed by anguish,
Crowds an excess of heavy thoughts;
Remembrance speechlessly unrolls
Its lengthy scroll before me;
And, reading through my life with loathing,
I tremble, curse, and bitterly complain,
And bitter tears pour from my eyes,
But the sad lines are not washed away.
—Pushkin[31]

Whether they killed him tomorrow morning or made a laughingstock of him, that is, left him to this life, in any case he was lost. Whether this disgraced woman killed herself in despair and shame or dragged out her pitiful existence, in any case she was lost...

So thought Laevsky, sitting at the table late at night and still rubbing his hands. The window suddenly opened with a bang, a strong wind burst into the room, and papers flew off the table. Laevsky closed the window and bent down to pick up the papers from the floor. He felt something new in his body, some sort of awkwardness that had not been there before, and he did not recognize his own movements; he walked warily, sticking out his elbows and jerking his shoulders, and when he sat down at the table, he again began rubbing his hands. His body had lost its suppleness.

On the eve of death, one must write to one's family.

Laevsky remembered that. He took up a pen and wrote in a shaky hand:

"Dear Mother!"

He wanted to write to his mother that, in the name of the merciful God in whom she believed, she should give shelter and the warmth of her tenderness to the unfortunate woman he had dishonored, lonely, poor, and weak; that she should forgive and forget everything, everything, everything, and with her sacrifice at least partially redeem her son's terrible sin; but he remembered how his mother, a stout, heavy old woman in a lace cap, went out to the garden in the morning, followed by a companion with a lapdog, how his mother shouted in a commanding voice at the gardener, at the servants, and how proud and arrogant her face was—he remembered it and crossed out the words he had written.

Lightning flashed brightly in all three windows, followed by a deafening, rolling clap of thunder, first muted, then rumbling and cracking, and so strong that the glass in the windows rattled. Laevsky got up, went to the window, and leaned his forehead against the glass. Outside there was a heavy, beautiful thunderstorm. On the horizon, lightning ceaselessly hurled itself in white ribbons from the clouds into the sea and lit up the high black waves far in the distance. Lightning flashed to right and left, and probably directly over the house as well.

"A thunderstorm!" whispered Laevsky; he felt a desire to pray to someone or something, if only to the lightning or the clouds. "Dear thunderstorm!"

He remembered how, in childhood, he had always run out to the garden bareheaded when there was a thunderstorm, and two fair-haired, blue-eyed little girls would chase after him, and the rain would drench them; they would laugh with delight, but when a strong clap of thunder rang out, the girls would press themselves trustfully to the boy, and he would cross himself and hasten to recite: "Holy, holy, holy . . ." Oh, where have you gone, in what sea have you drowned, you germs of a beautiful, pure life? He was no longer afraid of thunderstorms, did not love nature, had no God, all the trustful girls he had ever known had already been ruined by him or his peers, he had never planted a single tree in his own garden, nor grown a single blade of grass, and, living amidst the living, had never saved a single fly, but had only destroyed, ruined, and lied, lied...

"What in my past is not vice?" he kept asking himself, trying to clutch at some bright memory, as someone falling into an abyss clutches at a bush.

School? University? But that was a sham. He had been a poor student and had forgotten what he was taught. Serving society? That was also a sham, because he did nothing at work, received a salary gratis, and his service was a vile embezzlement for which one was not taken to court.

He had no need of the truth, and he was not seeking it; his conscience, beguiled by vice and lies, slept or was silent; like a foreigner, or an alien from another planet, he took no part in the common life of people, was indifferent to their sufferings, ideas, religions, knowledge, quests, struggles; he had not a single kind word for people, had never written a single useful, nonbanal line, had never done a groat's worth of anything for people, but only ate their bread, drank their wine, took away their wives, lived by their thoughts, and, to justify his contemptible, parasitic life before them and before himself, had always tried to make himself look higher and better than them... Lies, lies, lies...

He clearly recalled what he had seen that evening in Miuridov's house, and it gave him an unbearably creepy feeling of loathing and anguish. Kirilin and Atchmianov were disgusting, but they were merely continuing what he had begun; they were his accomplices and disciples. From a weak young woman who trusted him more than a brother, he had taken her husband, her circle of friends, and her native land, and had brought her here to the torrid heat, to fever, and to boredom;

day after day, like a mirror, she had had to reflect in herself his idleness, depravity, and lying—and that, that alone, had filled her weak, sluggish, pitiful life; then he had had enough of her, had begun to hate her, but had not had the courage to abandon her, and he had tried to entangle her in a tight mesh of lies, as in a spiderweb . . . These people had done the rest.

Laevsky now sat at the table, now went again to the window; now he put out the candle, now he lighted it again. He cursed himself aloud, wept, complained, asked forgiveness; several times he rushed to the desk in despair and wrote: "Dear Mother!"

Besides his mother, he had no family or relations; but how could his mother help him? And where was she? He wanted to rush to Nadezhda Fyodorovna, fall at her feet, kiss her hands and feet, beg for forgiveness, but she was his victim, and he was afraid of her, as if she was dead.

"My life is ruined!" he murmured, rubbing his hands. "Why am I still alive, my God! . . ."

He dislodged his own dim star from the sky, it fell, and its traces mingled with the night's darkness; it would never return to the sky, because life is given only once and is not repeated. If it had been possible to bring back the past days and years, he would have replaced the lies in them by truth, the idleness by work, the boredom by joy; he would have given back the purity to those from whom he had taken it, he would have found God and justice, but this was as impossible as putting a fallen star back into the sky. And the fact that it was impossible drove him to despair.

When the thunderstorm had passed, he sat by the open window and calmly thought of what was going to happen to him. Von Koren would probably kill him. The man's clear, cold worldview allowed for the destruction of the feeble and worthless; and if it betrayed him in the decisive moment, he would be helped by the hatred and squeamishness Laevsky inspired in him. But if he missed, or, to mock his hated adversary, only wounded him, or fired into the air, what was he to do then? Where was he to go?

"To Petersburg?" Laevsky asked himself. "But that would mean starting anew the old life I'm cursing. And he who seeks salvation in a change of place, like a migratory bird, will find nothing, because for him the earth is the same everywhere. Seek salvation in people? In whom and how? Samoilenko's kindness and magnanimity are no more saving than the deacon's laughter or von Koren's hatred. One must seek salvation only in oneself, and if one doesn't find it, then why waste time, one must kill oneself, that's all..."

The noise of a carriage was heard. Dawn was already breaking. The carriage drove past, turned, and, its wheels creaking in the wet sand, stopped near the house. Two men were sitting in the carriage.

"Wait, I'll be right there!" Laevsky said out the window. "I'm not asleep. Can it be time already?"

"Yes. Four o'clock. By the time we get there..."

Laevsky put on his coat and a cap, took some cigarettes in his pocket, and stopped to ponder; it seemed to him that something else had to be done. Outside, the seconds talked softly and the horses snorted, and these sounds, on a damp early morning, when everyone was asleep and the sky was barely light, filled Laevsky's soul with a despondency that was like a bad presentiment. He stood pondering for a while and then went to the bedroom.

Nadezhda Fyodorovna lay on her bed, stretched out, wrapped head and all in a plaid; she did not move and was reminiscent, especially by her head, of an Egyptian mummy. Looking at her in silence, Laevsky mentally asked her forgiveness and thought that if heaven was not empty and God was indeed in it, He would protect her, and if there was no God, let her perish, there was no need for her to live.

She suddenly jumped and sat up in her bed. Raising her pale face and looking with terror at Laevsky, she asked:

"Is that you? Is the thunderstorm over?"

"It's over."

She remembered, put both hands to her head, and her whole body shuddered.

"It's so hard for me!" she said. "If you only knew how hard it is for me! I was expecting you to kill me," she went on, narrowing her eyes, "or drive me out of the house into the rain and storm, but you put it off... put it off..."

He embraced her impulsively and tightly, covered her knees and hands with kisses, then, as she murmured something to him and shuddered from her memories, he smoothed her hair and, peering into her face, understood that this unfortunate, depraved woman was the only person who was close, dear, and irreplaceable to him.

When he left the house and was getting into the carriage, he wanted to come back home alive.

XVIII

THE DEACON GOT UP, dressed, took his thick, knobby walking stick, and quietly left the house. It was dark, and for the first moment, as he walked down the street, he did not even see his white stick; there was not a single star in the sky, and it looked as though it was going to rain again. There was a smell of wet sand and sea.

"If only the Chechens don't attack," thought the deacon, listening to his stick tapping the pavement and to the resounding and solitary sound this tapping made in the stillness of the night.

Once he left town, he began to see both the road and his stick; dim spots appeared here and there in the black sky, and soon one star peeped out and timidly winked its one eye. The deacon walked along the high rocky coast and did not see the sea; it was falling asleep below, and its invisible waves broke lazily and heavily against the shore and seemed to sigh: oof! And so slowly! One wave broke, the deacon had time to count eight steps, then another broke, and after six steps, a third. Just as before, nothing could be seen, and in the darkness, the lazy, sleepy noise of the sea could be heard, the infinitely far-off, unimaginable time could be heard when God hovered over chaos.

The deacon felt eerie. He thought God might punish him for keeping company with unbelievers and even going to watch their duel. The duel would be trifling, bloodless, ridiculous, but however it might be, it was a heathen spectacle, and for a clergyman to be present at it was altogether improper. He stopped and thought: shouldn't he go back? But strong, restless curiosity got the upper hand over his doubts, and he went on.

"Though they're unbelievers, they are good people and will be saved," he reassured himself. "They'll surely be saved!" he said aloud, lighting a cigarette.

By what measure must one measure people's qualities, to be able to judge them fairly? The deacon recalled his enemy, the inspector of the seminary, who believed in God, and did not fight duels, and lived in chastity, but used to feed the deacon bread with sand in it and once nearly tore his ear off. If human life was so unwisely formed that everyone in the seminary respected this cruel and dishonest inspector, who stole government flour, and prayed for his health and salvation, was it fair to keep away from such people as von Koren and Laevsky only because they were unbelievers? The deacon started mulling over this question but then recalled what a funny figure Samoilenko had cut that day, and that interrupted the course of his thoughts. How they would laugh tomorrow! The deacon imagined himself sitting behind a bush and spying on them, and when von Koren began boasting tomorrow at dinner, he, the deacon, would laugh and tell him all the details of the duel.

"How do you know all that?" the zoologist would ask.

"It just so happens. I stayed home, but I know."

It would be nice to write a funny description of the duel. His father-in-law would read it and laugh; hearing or reading something funny was better food for him than meat and potatoes.

The valley of the Yellow River opened out. The rain had made the river wider and angrier, and it no longer rumbled as before, but roared. Dawn was breaking. The gray, dull morning, and the clouds racing westward to catch up with the thunderhead, and the mountains girded with mist, and the wet trees—it all seemed ugly and angry to the deacon. He washed in a brook, recited his morning prayers, and wished he could have some tea and the hot puffs with sour cream served every morning at his father-in-law's table. He thought of his deaconess and "The Irretrievable," which she played on the piano. What sort of woman was she? They had introduced the deacon to her, arranged things, and married him to her in a week; he had lived with her for less than a month and had been ordered here, so that he had not yet figured out what kind of person she was. But all the same, he was slightly bored without her.

"I must write her a little letter..." he thought.

The flag on the dukhan was rain-soaked and drooping, and the dukhan itself, with its wet roof, seemed darker and lower than it had before. A cart stood by the door. Kerbalai, a couple of Abkhazians, and a young Tartar woman in balloon trousers, probably Kerbalai's wife or daughter, were bringing sacks of something out of the dukhan and putting them in the cart on cornhusks. By the cart stood a pair of oxen, their heads lowered. After loading the sacks, the Abkhazians and the Tartar woman began covering them with straw, and Kerbalai hastily began hitching up the donkeys.

"Contraband, probably," thought the deacon.

Here was the fallen tree with its dried needles, here was

the black spot from the fire. He recalled the picnic in all its details, the fire, the singing of the Abkhazians, the sweet dreams of a bishopric and a procession with the cross ... The Black River had grown blacker and wider from the rain. The deacon cautiously crossed the flimsy bridge, which the muddy waves already reached with their crests, and climbed the ladder into the drying shed.

"A fine head!" he thought, stretching out on the straw and recalling von Koren. "A good head, God grant him health. Only there's cruelty in him ..."

Why did he hate Laevsky, and Laevsky him? Why were they going to fight a duel? If they had known the same poverty as the deacon had known since childhood, if they had been raised in the midst of ignorant, hard-hearted people, greedy for gain, who reproached you for a crust of bread, coarse and uncouth of behavior, who spat on the floor and belched over dinner and during prayers, if they had not been spoiled since childhood by good surroundings and a select circle of people, how they would cling to each other, how eagerly they would forgive each other's shortcomings and value what each of them did have. For there are so few even outwardly decent people in the world! True, Laevsky was crackbrained, dissolute, strange, but he wouldn't steal, wouldn't spit loudly on the floor, wouldn't reproach his wife: "You stuff yourself, but you don't want to work," wouldn't beat a child with a harness strap or feed his servants putrid salt beef—wasn't that enough for him to be treated with tolerance? Besides, he was the first to suffer from his own shortcomings, like a sick man from his sores. Instead of seeking, out of boredom or some sort of misunderstanding, for degeneracy, extinction, heredity, and other incomprehensible things in each other, wouldn't it be better for them to descend a little lower and direct their hatred and wrath to where whole streets resound with the groans of coarse ignorance, greed, reproach, impurity, curses, female shrieks ...

There was the sound of an equipage, and it interrupted the deacon's thoughts. He peeked out the door and saw a carriage, and in it three people: Laevsky, Sheshkovsky, and the head of the post and telegraph office.

"Stop!" said Sheshkovsky.

All three got out of the carriage and looked at each other.

"They're not here yet," said Sheshkovsky, shaking mud off himself. "So, then! While the jury's still out, let's go and find a suitable spot. There's hardly room enough to turn around here."

They went further up the river and soon disappeared from sight. The Tartar coachman got into the carriage, lolled his head on his shoulder, and fell asleep. Having waited for about ten minutes, the deacon came out of the drying shed and, taking off his black hat so as not to be noticed, cowering and glancing around, began to make his way along the bank among the bushes and strips of corn; big drops fell on him from the trees and bushes, the grass and corn were wet.

"What a shame!" he muttered, hitching up his wet and dirty skirts. "If I'd known, I wouldn't have come."

Soon he heard voices and saw people. Laevsky, hunched over, his hands tucked into his sleeves, was rapidly pacing up and down a small clearing; his seconds stood just by the bank and rolled cigarettes.

"Strange . . ." thought the deacon, not recognizing Laevsky's gait. "Looks like an old man."

"How impolite on their part!" said the postal official, looking at his watch. "Maybe for a learned man it's a fine thing to be late, but in my opinion it's swinishness."

Sheshkovsky, a fat man with a black beard, listened and said:

"They're coming."

XIX

"THE FIRST TIME in my life I've seen it! How nice!" said von Koren, emerging into the clearing and holding out both arms to the east. "Look: green rays!"

Two green rays stretched out from behind the mountains in the east, and it was indeed beautiful. The sun was rising.

"Good morning!" the zoologist went on, nodding to Laevsky's seconds. "I'm not late?"

Behind him came his seconds, two very young officers of the same height, Boiko and Govorovsky, in white tunics, and the lean, unsociable Dr. Ustimovich, who was carrying a bundle of something in one hand and put the other behind him; as usual, he was holding his cane up along his spine. Setting the bundle on the ground and not greeting anyone, he sent his other hand behind his back and began pacing out the clearing.

Laevsky felt the weariness and awkwardness of a man who might die soon and therefore attracted general attention. He would have liked to be killed quickly or else taken home. He was now seeing a sunrise for the first time in his life; this early morning, the green rays, the dampness, and the people in wet boots seemed extraneous to his life, unnecessary, and they embarrassed him; all this had no connection with the night he had lived through, with his thoughts, and with the feeling of guilt, and therefore he would gladly have left without waiting for the duel.

Von Koren was noticeably agitated and tried to conceal it, pretending that he was interested most of all in the green rays. The seconds were confused and kept glancing at each other as if asking why they were there and what they were to do.

"I suppose, gentlemen, that there's no need to go further," said Sheshkovsky. "Here is all right."

"Yes, of course," agreed von Koren.

Silence ensued. Ustimovich, as he paced, suddenly turned sharply to Laevsky and said in a low voice, breathing in his face:

"They probably haven't had time to inform you of my conditions. Each side pays me fifteen roubles, and in case of the death of one of the adversaries, the one who is left alive pays the whole thirty."

Laevsky had made this man's acquaintance earlier, but only now did he see distinctly for the first time his dull eyes, stiff mustache, and lean, consumptive neck: a moneylender, not a doctor! His breath had an unpleasant, beefy smell.

"It takes all kinds to make a world," thought Laevsky and replied:

"Very well."

The doctor nodded and again began pacing, and it was clear that he did not need the money at all, but was asking for it simply out of hatred. Everyone felt that it was time to begin, or to end what had been begun, yet they did not begin or end, but walked about, stood, and smoked. The young officers, who were present at a duel for the first time in their lives and now had little faith in this civil and, in their opinion, unnecessary duel, attentively examined their tunics and smoothed their sleeves. Sheshkovsky came up to them and said quietly:

"Gentlemen, we should make every effort to keep the duel from taking place. They must be reconciled."

He blushed and went on:

"Last night Kirilin came to see me and complained that Laevsky had caught him last night with Nadezhda Fyodorovna and all that."

"Yes, we also know about that," said Boiko.

"Well, so you see . . . Laevsky's hands are trembling and all that . . . He won't even be able to hold up a pistol now. It would be as inhuman to fight with him as with a drunk man or someone with typhus. If the reconciliation doesn't take place, then, gentlemen, we must at least postpone the duel or something... It's such a devilish thing, I don't even want to look."

"Speak with von Koren."

"I don't know the rules of dueling, devil take them all, and I don't want to know them; maybe he'll think Laevsky turned coward and sent me to him. But anyhow, he can think what he likes, I'll go and speak with him."

Irresolutely, limping slightly, as though his foot had gone to sleep, Sheshkovsky went over to von Koren, and as he walked and grunted, his whole figure breathed indolence.

"There's something I've got to tell you, sir," he began, attentively studying the flowers on the zoologist's shirt. "It's confidential... I don't know the rules of dueling, devil take them all, and I don't want to know them, and I'm reasoning not as a second and all that but as a human being, that's all."

"Right. So?"

"When seconds suggest making peace, usually nobody listens to them, looking on it as a formality. Amour propre and nothing more. But I humbly beg you to pay attention to Ivan Andreich. He's not at all in a normal state today, so to speak, not in his right mind, and quite pitiful. A misfortune has befallen him. I can't bear gossip," Sheshkovsky blushed and looked around, "but in view of the duel, I find it necessary to tell you. Last night, in Miuridov's house, he found his lady with... a certain gentleman."

"How revolting!" murmured the zoologist; he turned pale, winced, and spat loudly: "Pah!"

His lower lip trembled; he stepped away from Sheshkovsky, not wishing to hear any more, and, as if he had accidentally sampled something bitter, again spat loudly, and for the first time that morning looked at Laevsky with hatred. His agitation and awkwardness passed; he shook his head and said loudly:

"Gentlemen, what are we waiting for, may I ask? Why don't we begin?"

Sheshkovsky exchanged glances with the officers and shrugged his shoulders.

"Gentlemen!" he said loudly, not addressing anyone. "Gentlemen! We suggest that you make peace!"

"Let's get through the formalities quickly," said von Koren. "We've already talked about making peace. What's the next formality now? Let's hurry up, gentlemen, time won't wait."

"But we still insist on making peace," Sheshkovsky said in a guilty voice, like a man forced to interfere in other people's business; he blushed, put his hand to his heart, and went on: "Gentlemen, we see no causal connection between the insult and the duel. An offense that we, in our human weakness, sometimes inflict on each other and a duel have nothing in common. You're university and cultivated people, and, of course, you yourselves see nothing in dueling but an outdated and empty formality and all that. We look at it the same way, otherwise we wouldn't have come, because we can't allow people to shoot at each other in our presence, that's all." Sheshkovsky wiped the sweat from his face and went on: "Let's put an end to your misunderstanding, gentlemen, offer each other your hands, and go home and drink to peace. Word of honor, gentlemen!"

Von Koren was silent. Laevsky, noticing that they were looking at him, said:

"I have nothing against Nikolai Vassilievich. If he finds me to blame, I'm ready to apologize to him."

Von Koren became offended.

"Obviously, gentlemen," he said, "you would like Mr. Laevsky to return home a magnanimous and chivalrous man, but I cannot give you and him that pleasure. And there was no need to get up early and go seven miles out of town only to drink to peace, have a bite to eat, and explain to me that dueling is an outdated formality. A duel is a duel, and it ought not to be made more stupid and false than it is in reality. I want to fight!"

Silence ensued. Officer Boiko took two pistols from a box; one was handed to von Koren, the other to Laevsky, and after that came perplexity, which briefly amused the zoologist and the seconds. It turned out that of all those present, not one had been at a duel even once in his life, and no one knew exactly how they should stand and what the seconds should say and do. But then Boiko remembered and, smiling, began to explain.

"Gentlemen, who remembers how it's described in Lermontov?" von Koren asked, laughing. "In Turgenev, too, Bazarov exchanged shots with somebody or other . . ."

"What is there to remember?" Ustimovich said impatiently, stopping. "Measure out the distance—that's all."

And he made three paces, as if showing them how to measure. Boiko counted off the paces, and his comrade drew his saber and scratched the ground at the extreme points to mark the barrier.

In the general silence, the adversaries took their places.

"Moles," recalled the deacon, who was sitting in the bushes.

Sheshkovsky was saying something, Boiko was explaining something again, but Laevsky did not hear or, more precisely, heard but did not understand. When the time for it came, he cocked and raised the heavy, cold pistol, barrel up. He forgot to unbutton his coat, and it felt very tight in the shoulder and armpit, and his arm was rising as awkwardly as if the sleeve was made of tin. He remembered his hatred yesterday for the swarthy forehead and curly hair, and thought that even yesterday, in a moment of intense hatred and wrath, he could not have shot at a man. Fearing that the bullet might somehow accidentally hit von Koren, he raised the pistol higher and higher, and felt that this much too ostentatious magnanimity was neither delicate nor magnanimous, but he could not and would not do otherwise. Looking at the pale, mockingly smiling face of von Koren, who had evidently been sure from the very beginning that his adversary would fire into the air, Laevsky thought that soon, thank God, it would all be over, and that he had only to squeeze the trigger harder . . .

There was a strong kick in his shoulder, a shot rang out, and in the mountains the echo answered: ka-bang!

Von Koren, too, cocked his pistol and glanced in the direction of Ustimovich, who was pacing as before, his hands thrust behind him, paying no attention to anything.

"Doctor," said the zoologist, "kindly do not walk like a pendulum. You flash in my eyes."

The doctor stopped. Von Koren started aiming at Laevsky.

"It's all over!" thought Laevsky.

The barrel of the pistol pointing straight at his face, the expression of hatred and contempt in the pose and the whole figure of von Koren, and this murder that a decent man was about to commit in broad daylight in the presence of decent people, and this silence, and the unknown force that made Laevsky stand there and not run away—how mysterious, and incomprehensible, and frightening it all was! The time von Koren took to aim seemed longer than a night to Laevsky. He glanced imploringly at the seconds; they did not move and were pale.

"Shoot quickly!" thought Laevsky, and felt that his pale, quivering, pitiful face must arouse still greater hatred in von Koren.

"Now I'll kill him," thought von Koren, aiming at the forehead and already feeling the trigger with his finger. "Yes, of course, I'll kill him . . ."

"He'll kill him!" a desperate cry was suddenly heard somewhere very nearby.

Just then the shot rang out. Seeing that Laevsky was

standing in the same place and did not fall, everyone looked in the direction the cry had come from, and saw the deacon. Pale, his wet hair stuck to his forehead and cheeks, all wet and dirty, he was standing on the other bank in the corn, smiling somehow strangely and waving his wet hat. Sheshkovsky laughed with joy, burst into tears, and walked away . . .

XX

A LITTLE LATER, von Koren and the deacon came together at the little bridge. The deacon was agitated, breathed heavily, and avoided looking him in the eye. He was ashamed both of his fear and of his dirty, wet clothes.

"It seemed to me that you wanted to kill him . . ." he mumbled. "How contrary it is to human nature! Unnatural to such a degree!"

"How did you get here, though?" asked the zoologist.

"Don't ask!" the deacon waved his hand. "The unclean one led me astray: go, yes, go . . . So I went and almost died of fright in the corn. But now, thank God, thank God . . . I'm quite pleased with you," the deacon went on mumbling. "And our grandpa tarantula will be pleased . . . Funny, so funny! Only I beg you insistently not to tell anyone I was here, or else I may get it in the neck from my superiors. They'll say: the deacon acted as a second."

"Gentlemen!" said von Koren. "The deacon asks you not to tell anybody you saw him here. He may get in trouble."

"How contrary it is to human nature!" sighed the deacon. "Forgive me magnanimously, but you had such a look on your face that I thought you were certainly going to kill him."

"I was strongly tempted to finish the scoundrel off," said von Koren, "but you shouted right then, and I missed. However, this whole procedure is revolting to someone unaccustomed to it, and it's made me tired, Deacon. I feel terribly weak. Let's go . . ."

"No, kindly allow me to go on foot. I've got to dry out, I'm all wet and chilly."

"Well, you know best," the weakened zoologist said in a weary voice, getting into the carriage and closing his eyes. "You know best . . ."

While they were walking around the carriages and getting into them, Kerbalai stood by the road and, holding his stomach with both hands, kept bowing low and showing his teeth; he thought the gentlemen had come to enjoy nature and drink tea, and did not understand why they were getting into the carriages. In the general silence, the train started, and the only one left by the dukhan was the deacon.

"Went dukhan, drank tea," he said to Kerbalai. "Mine wants eat."

Kerbalai spoke Russian well, but the deacon thought the Tartar would understand him better if he spoke to him in broken Russian.

"Fried eggs, gave cheese . . ."

"Come in, come in, pope," Kerbalai said, bowing, "I'll give you everything . . . There's cheese, there's wine . . . Eat whatever you like."

"What's God in Tartar?" the deacon asked as he went into the dukhan.

"Your God and my God are all the same," said Kerbalai, not understanding him. "God is one for everybody, only people are different. Some are Russian, some are Turks, or some are English—there are many kinds of people, but God is one."

"Very good, sir. If all people worship one God, why do you Muslims look upon Christians as your eternal enemies?"

"Why get angry?" said Kerbalai, clasping his stomach with both hands. "You're a pope, I'm a Muslim, you say you want to eat, I give . . . Only the rich man sorts out which God is yours, which is mine, but for a poor man, it's all the same. Eat, please."

While a theological discussion was going on in the dukhan, Laevsky drove home and remembered how eerie it had been to drive out at dawn, when the road, the cliffs, and the mountains were wet and dark and the unknown future seemed as frightening as an abyss with no bottom to be seen, while now the raindrops hanging on the grass and rocks sparkled in the sun like diamonds, nature smiled joyfully, and the frightening future was left behind. He kept glancing at the sullen, tear-stained face of Sheshkovsky and ahead at the two carriages in which von Koren, his seconds, and the doctor rode, and it seemed to him as though they were all coming back from a cemetery where they had just buried a difficult, unbearable man who had interfered with all their lives.

"It's all over," he thought about his past, carefully stroking his neck with his fingers.

On the right side of his neck, near the collar, he had a small swelling, as long and thick as a little finger, and he felt pain, as if someone had passed a hot iron over his neck. It was a contusion from a bullet.

Then, when he got home, a long, strange day, sweet and foggy as oblivion, wore on for him. Like a man released from prison or the hospital, he peered at long-familiar objects and was surprised that the tables, the windows, the chairs, the light and the sea aroused a living, childlike joy in him, such as he had not experienced for a long, long time. Nadezhda Fyodorovna, pale and grown very thin, did not understand his meek voice and strange gait; she hurriedly told him everything that had happened to her . . . It seemed to her that he probably listened poorly and did not understand her, and that if he learned everything, he would curse and kill her, yet he listened to her, stroked her face and hair, looked into her eyes, and said:

"I have no one but you . . ."

Then they sat for a long time in the front garden, pressed to each other, and said nothing, or else, dreaming aloud of their happy future life, they uttered short, abrupt phrases, and it seemed to him that he had never spoken so lengthily and beautifully.

XXI

A LITTLE MORE than three months went by.

The day von Koren had appointed for his departure came. Cold rain had been falling in big drops since early morning, a northeast wind was blowing, and the sea churned itself up in big waves. People said that in such weather the steamer could hardly put into the roads. According to the schedule, it should have come after nine, but von Koren, who went out to the embankment at noon and after dinner, saw nothing through his binoculars but gray waves and rain obscuring the horizon.

Towards the end of the day, the rain stopped, and the wind began to drop noticeably. Von Koren was already reconciled with the thought that he was not to leave that day, and he sat down to play chess with Samoilenko; but when it grew dark, the orderly reported that lights had appeared on the sea and a rocket had been seen.

Von Koren began to hurry. He shouldered a bag, kissed Samoilenko and then the deacon, went around all the rooms quite needlessly, said good-bye to the orderly and the cook, and went out feeling as though he had forgotten something at the doctor's or at his own place. He went down the street side by side with Samoilenko, followed by the deacon with a box, and behind them all came the orderly with two suitcases. Only Samoilenko and the orderly could make out the dim lights on the sea; the others looked into the darkness and saw nothing. The steamer had stopped far from shore.

"Quick, quick," von Koren urged. "I'm afraid it will leave!"

Passing by the three-windowed little house Laevsky had moved into soon after the duel, von Koren could not help looking in the window. Laevsky, bent over, was sitting at a desk, his back to the window, and writing.

"I'm astonished," the zoologist said softly. "How he's put the screws to himself!"

"Yes, it's worthy of astonishment," sighed Samoilenko. "He sits like that from morning till evening, sits and works. He wants to pay his debts. And brother, he lives worse than a beggar!"

Half a minute passed in silence. The zoologist, the doctor, and the deacon stood by the window, and they all looked at Laevsky.

"So he never left here, poor fellow," said Samoilenko. "Remember how he fussed about?"

"Yes, he's really put the screws to himself," repeated von Koren. "His marriage, this all-day work for a crust of bread, some new expression in his face, and even his gait—it's all extraordinary to such a degree that I don't even know what to call it." The zoologist took Samoilenko by the sleeve and went on with agitation in his voice: "Tell him and his wife that I was astonished at them as I was leaving, wished them well . . . and ask him, if it's possible, not to think ill of me. He knows me. He knows that if I could have foreseen this change then, I might have become his best friend."

"Go in to him, say good-bye."

"No. It's awkward."

"Why? God knows, maybe you'll never see him again."

The zoologist thought a little and said:

"That's true."

Samoilenko tapped softly on the window with his finger. Laevsky gave a start and turned to look.

"Vanya, Nikolai Vassilyich wishes to say good-bye to you," said Samoilenko. "He's just leaving."

Laevsky got up from the desk and went to the front hall to open the door. Samoilenko, von Koren, and the deacon came in.

"I've come for a moment," the zoologist began, taking off his galoshes in the front hall and already regretting that he had given way to his feelings and come in uninvited. ("As if I'm forcing myself on him," he thought, "and that's stupid.") "Forgive me for bothering you," he said, following Laevsky into his room, "but I'm just leaving, and I felt drawn to you. God knows if we'll ever see each other again."

"I'm very glad . . . I humbly beg you," said Laevsky, and he awkwardly moved chairs for his visitors, as if he wished to bar their way, and stopped in the middle of the room, rubbing his hands.

"I should have left the witnesses outside," thought von Koren, and he said firmly:

"Don't think ill of me, Ivan Andreich. To forget the past is, of course, impossible, it is all too sad, and I haven't come here to apologize or to insist that I'm not to blame. I acted sincerely and have not changed my convictions since . . . True, as I now see, to my great joy, I was mistaken concerning you, but one can stumble even on a smooth road, and such is human fate: if you're not mistaken in the main thing, you'll be mistaken in the details. No one knows the real truth."

"Yes, no one knows the truth . . ." said Laevsky.

"Well, good-bye . . . God grant you all good things."

Von Koren gave Laevsky his hand; he shook it and bowed.

"So don't think ill of me," said von Koren. "Give my greetings to your wife, and tell her I was very sorry I couldn't say good-bye to her."

"She's here."

Laevsky went to the door and said into the other room:

"Nadya, Nikolai Vassilievich wishes to say good-bye to you."

Nadezhda Fyodorovna came in; she stopped by the door and looked timidly at the visitors. Her face was guilty and frightened, and she held her arms like a schoolgirl who is being reprimanded.

"I'm just leaving, Nadezhda Fyodorovna," said von Koren, "and I've come to say good-bye."

She offered him her hand irresolutely, and Laevsky bowed.

"How pitiful they both are, though!" thought von Koren. "They don't come by this life cheaply."

"I'll be in Moscow and Petersburg," he asked, "do you need to have anything sent from there?"

"Need anything?" said Nadezhda Fyodorovna, and she exchanged alarmed glances with her husband. "Nothing, I believe..."

"No, nothing..." said Laevsky, rubbing his hands. "Say hello for us."

Von Koren did not know what else could or needed to be said, yet earlier, as he was coming in, he thought he would say a great many good, warm, and significant things. He silently shook hands with Laevsky and his wife and went out with a heavy feeling.

"What people!" the deacon was saying in a low voice, walking behind. "My God, what people! Truly, the right hand of God planted this vineyard! Lord, Lord! One defeated thousands and the other tens of thousands.[32] Nikolai Vassilyich," he said ecstatically, "know that today you have defeated the greatest human enemy—pride!"

"Come now, Deacon! What kind of victors are we? Victors look like eagles, but he's pitiful, timid, downtrodden, he keeps bowing like a Chinese doll, and I ... I feel sad."

There was the sound of footsteps behind them. It was Laevsky catching up to see them off. On the pier stood the orderly with the two suitcases, and a little further off, four oarsmen.

"It's really blowing, though...brr!" said Samoilenko. "Must be a whale of a storm out at sea—aie, aie! It's not a good time to be going, Kolya."

"I'm not afraid of seasickness."

"That's not the point... These fools may capsize you. You ought to have gone in the agent's skiff. Where's the agent's skiff?" he shouted to the oarsmen.

"Gone, Your Excellency."

"And the customs skiff?"

"Also gone."

"Why wasn't it announced?" Samoilenko got angry. "Dunderheads!"

"Never mind, don't worry..." said von Koren. "Well, good-bye. God keep you."

Samoilenko embraced von Koren and crossed him three times.

"Don't forget me, Kolya...Write...We'll expect you next spring."

"Good-bye, Deacon," said von Koren, shaking the deacon's hand. "Thanks for the company and the good conversation. Think about the expedition."

"Lord, yes, even to the ends of the earth!" laughed the deacon. "Am I against it?"

Von Koren recognized Laevsky in the darkness and silently gave him his hand. The oarsmen were already standing below, holding the boat, which kept knocking against the pilings, though the pier sheltered it from the big swells. Von Koren went down the ladder, jumped into the boat, and sat by the tiller.

"Write!" Samoilenko shouted to him. "Take care of yourself!"

"No one knows the real truth," thought Laevsky, turning up the collar of his coat and tucking his hands into his sleeves.

The boat briskly rounded the pier and headed into the open. It disappeared among the waves, but shot up at once out of the deep hole onto a high hill, so that it was possible to make out the people and even the oars. The boat went ahead about six yards and was thrown back four.

"Write!" shouted Samoilenko. "What the deuce makes you go in such weather!"

"Yes, no one knows the real truth..." thought Laevsky, looking with anguish at the restless, dark sea.

"The boat is thrown back," he thought, "it makes two steps forward and one step back, but the oarsmen are stubborn, they work the oars tirelessly and do not fear the high waves. The boat goes on and on, now it can no longer be seen, and in half an hour the oarsmen will clearly see the steamer's lights, and in an hour they'll already be by the steamer's ladder. So it is in life... In search of the truth, people make two steps forward and one step back. Sufferings, mistakes, and the tedium of life throw them back, but the thirst for truth and a stubborn will drive them on and on. And who knows? Maybe they'll row their way to the real truth..."

"Good-by-y-ye!" shouted Samoilenko.

"No sight or sound of them," said the deacon. "Safe journey!"

It began to drizzle.

1891

NOTES

1. Russian civil servants had official uniforms similar to the military.

2. State councillor was the fifth in the table of ranks. The table of fourteen civil administrative ranks, numbered highest to lowest, was established in 1722 by emporer Peter the Great (1672–1725). Only those of the fourth rank and higher, which conferred hereditary nobility, were entitled to be called "Your Excellency."

3. Ivan Turgenev (1818–83) introduced this term in his *Diary of a Superfluous Man* (1850); it came to typify intellectuals from the 1840s to the '60s, but by Laevsky's time was rather outdated. The eponymous hero of *Evgeny Onegin* (1823–30), a novel in verse by Alexander Pushkin (1799–1837); Chatsky, the protagonist of the comedy *Woe from Wit*, by Alexander Griboedov (1795–1829); and Pechorin, the protagonist of the novel *A Hero of Our Time* (1840), by Mikhail Lermontov (1814–41), were precursors of Turgenev's character, as were some of Byron's heroes.

4. Herbert Spencer (1820–1903) was an influential British philosopher who applied the theory of evolution to social life in a doctrine sometimes known as Social Darwinism.

5. Nevsky Prospect is the central thoroughfare of Petersburg, very popular for strolling and being seen, and the subject of much literature, most notably the story "Nevsky Prospect," by Nikolai Gogol (1809–52).

6. Vasily V. Vereshchagin (1842–1904), a soldier and traveler as well as an eminent painter, was best known for his military canvases, which portrayed the brutality rather than the glory of war. He was killed in the Russo-Japanese war.

7. The Order of Saint Vladimir was established by the empress Catherine the Great (1729–96) in 1792, in honor of Grand Prince Vladimir (960–1015), who converted Russia to Christianity in 988. It was both a civil and a military order; the military form of the decoration had a cross with crossed swords and a black and red bow.

8. The zemstvo was a local assembly for provincial self-government instituted by the legal reforms of the emperor Alexander II in 1864 and abolished by the 1917 revolution.

9. See note 3 above. Bazarov is the hero of Turgenev's novel *Fathers and Children* (1862) and the first "nihilist" in Russian literature.

10. The German philosopher Arthur Schopenhauer (1788–1860) was one of the greatest and most influential thinkers of the nineteenth century. His major work is *The World As Will and Representation* (1818).

11. The distinguished University of Dorpat, now Tartu, the second largest city of Estonia, was founded in 1632 by Gustavus II of Sweden. After many vicissitudes, it was reopened in 1802 under a charter from the Russian emperor Alexander I (the territory then being annexed to Russia), with German as its language of instruction.

12. In the Orthodox Church, a metropolitan is a bishop who oversees a large ecclesiastical territory known as a metropolis. He ranks above an archbishop and below a patriarch.

13. In Russia, a dacha can be anything from a large summer house to a rented room in the country or at the seashore, but the "dacha season," from June to August, with its long nights, also implies a special form of social life, with visits, evening parties, theatricals, and so on.

14. A dukhan is a tavern run by local Caucasian people who were traditionally Muslim but catered to the tastes of their Russian rulers.

15. A hieromonk is an Orthodox monk who is also a priest.

16. Baba Yaga, the fearsome witch of Russian fairy tales, lives in a hut on chicken's legs that spins round and round when someone approaches it.

17. A famous passage from Canto 3 of Pushkin's long poem *Poltava* (1829), beginning: "Quiet is the Ukrainian night . . ."

18. An archimandrite is the superior of an Orthodox monastery. A bishop traditionally wears a mitre and a panagia ("all-holy" in Greek, an icon of the Mother of God with the child Christ on a chain around the neck) and blesses the faithful with a double candlestick (dikíri) in one hand, signifying the two natures of Christ, and a triple candlestick (trikíri) in the other, signifying the three persons of the Trinity. During the liturgy, he speaks the line Chekhov quotes here, after which the choir sings the trisagion (the "thrice holy" supplication: "Holy God, Holy Mighty, Holy Immortal, have mercy on us!").

19. A line from Pushkin's *Evgeny Onegin*, Chapter 1, Stanza XVI.

20. The fig is a contemptuous gesture (*figue* in French, *fica* in Italian) made by inserting the thumb between the first and second fingers of the fist; in Russia it has been developed in various specific forms: the fig under the nose, the fig with butter, the fig in the pocket.

21. Words from the Orthodox funeral or memorial service ("Give rest, O Lord, to the soul of thy servant who has fallen asleep").

22. The Welsh-born journalist Henry Morton Stanley (1841–1904), who was sent as a *New York Times* reporter to find the famous Scottish explorer of Africa, David Livingstone (1813–73), who had not been heard from for five years and was presumed dead. Stanley set out with his expedition in 1869 and in 1871 found Dr. Livingstone, frail but alive.

23. A phrase ultimately derived from an episode in Plutarch's life of Caesar. As the young Caesar was crossing the Alps on his way to Spain, he passed through a wretched village inhabited by a few half-starved people. When his companions began to make fun of them, Caesar replied: "For my part, I had rather be the first man among these fellows than the second man in Rome."

24. Count Alexei A. Arakcheev (1769–1834), Russian soldier and statesman, was entrusted by the emperor Paul I (1754–1801) with the reform of the army, a task he carried out with notoriously ruthless discipline.

25. A reference to the Gospels: "And whosoever shall offend one of these little ones that believe in me, it is better for him that a millstone were hanged about his neck, and he were cast into the sea" (Mark 9:42; see also Matthew 18:6).

26. The litanies of the Orthodox liturgy include a petition "for a good defense before the dread Judgment Seat of Christ" at the Last Judgment.

27. Rudin, a restless, ineffectual idealist of the 1840s, is the hero of the novel of the same name (1856) by Ivan Turgenev (see note 3 above). He is killed on the barricades in Paris during the revolution of 1848.

28. Nikolai Leskov (1831–95), one of the greatest masters of Russian prose, published his "Legend of the Conscientious Danila" in 1888.

29. See the epistle of James 2:17: "Even so faith, if it hath not works, is dead, being alone," and Paul's epistle to the Galatians 2:16: "a man is not justified by the works of the law, but by the faith of Jesus Christ."

30. The Peter-and-Paul fortress, the oldest building in Petersburg, was a prison of formidable reputation, reserved mainly for political criminals.

31. The lines are from the poem "Remembrance" (1828).

32. See I Samuel 18:7: "Saul hath slain his thousands, and David his ten thousands."